BREAD FOR THE BAKER'S CHILD

BREAD
FOR THE
BAKER'S CHILD

A NOVEL

Joseph Caldwell

Sarabande  Books

LOUISVILLE, KENTUCKY

No part of this book may be reproduced without written permission of the publisher. Please direct inquiries to:

> Managing Editor
> Sarabande Books, Inc.
> 2234 Dundee Road, Suite 200
> Louisville, KY 40205

LIBRARY OF CONGRESS CATALOGING–IN–PUBLICATION DATA

Caldwell, Joseph.
    Bread for the baker's child : a novel / by Joseph Caldwell.
    p.   cm.
  ISBN 1-889330-65-5 (cloth : alk. paper) — ISBN 1-889330-66-3 (pbk. : alk. paper)
I. Title.
PS3553.A396 B74 2002
813'.54—dc21   2001020567

Cover photograph by Clarence Diffenderfer

The author would like to thank the editors of *Ambit* and *The Antioch Review*, where portions of this novel previously appeared in somewhat different form.

Cover and text design by Charles Casey Martin

Manufactured in the United States of America
This book is printed on acid-free paper.

Sarabande Books is a nonprofit literary organization.

Publication of this book was funded in part by a grant from the Kentucky Arts Council, a state agency of the Education, Arts and Humanities Cabinet.

FIRST EDITION

To
Van Varner

"No one is worse shod than the shoemaker's child."

—OLD PROVERB

ONE

Sister Rachel, teacup in hand, stood at the great window of the mansion and looked out toward the abandoned shoe factory on the far side of the river. She was wondering if she should tell the Mother General, asleep, dying in the bed behind her, that her brother—Rachel's— was not only in jail, sentenced to four years at Chevaren medium-security prison, but was revealed to be the heretofore anonymous benefactor who had donated to their Order more than a million dollars, all of it stolen money.

She took a sip of tea. It had begun to cool, and the lemon slice she'd squeezed into it floated under the tip of her nose, then slid alongside her upper lip. She put the cup back onto the saucer. Some pieces of lemon pulp were floating around on top of the tea. Or maybe they were dust motes. She began to speculate, trying to decide: pulp or dust. Or were they microbes, invisible microscopic bacteria, bloated now into visibility? Rachel's speculations came more from a habit of bewilderment than from any fear of contamination. She had, as usual, a wish to know and to understand, even though experience had told her that this was a wish not always granted and a hope seldom fulfilled.

What seemed to be a piece of pulp floated toward a dust mote. The two of them joined, then stuck themselves to the side of the cup. Rachel knew she should stop staring, that she should go ahead and make up her mind: should she trouble Mother with her news or not? She took a fair-sized gulp of the tea and punched her fist down into the pocket of her smock, crunching the letter and the check. The check was for one hundred eighty-seven dollars and thirty-two cents. The letter was from Mr. Thomas Tallent of the firm Barbour, Tallent, Dempsey, and Hayes. Both Mr. Tallent and the firm were famous throughout the Order. From them, over the years, had come the benevolent checks, made out in dizzying sums, the actual donor never to be known. But the letter in her smock pocket now informed her that this closed out her brother's account. The name of Thomas Tallent, the firm of Barbour, Tallent, Dempsey, and Hayes appearing now could not be a coincidence, especially since the letter also told her that her brother, Phillip Manrahan, was in jail, and for embezzlement. But the amount mentioned at the trial—uncontested—was, according to Mr. Tallent, a mere (mere!) twenty-three thousand dollars. Rachel didn't know what to think. Surely the Mother General would explain everything.

But if the money—the million and more—had been stolen, would they have to give it back? It was built into the new wing of the college library, plastered and painted into the walls of several schools, nailed onto the roofs of three different convents, and locked into the plumbing of the Motherhouse. Through its pipes had passed the water to make the tea she was, at this moment, holding in her hand.

Rachel looked out the window trying to decide what to do. The factory, high on its own bluff, had, after all, an unending fascination for her. Its design had been inspired, according to legend, by a Roman villa, replicated now in glass and steel instead of stucco and stone, but with four big-bellied urns, one at each corner of the roof, like offerings to the gods of plenty, an attempt on the part of the shoe baron to insinuate the splendors of antiquity into the squalors of the Industrial Revolution. In actuality, the factory resembled, quite rightly, a shoe box, oblong, its height in fine proportion to its length and width. But it was made mostly of windows, of glass, as if claiming a lineage going back to Cinderella's slipper when shoes were involved with magic and central to the workings of romance.

But with no lasts, no lathes, no hammers, with no poundings, no whirrings, no clankings, the factory, in its silence, had become yet another empty dwelling committed to the slow process of surrender. Sumac had already broken through the asphalt near the docking platforms and along the factory foundations. Oak, maple, and sycamore—and a possible cottonwood—had staked their claims in the parking lot, and there was a sapling, close to the edge of the bluff, that Rachel had hoped might be an elm. If it were, it would announce the end of the blight, the return of the great fountainlike tree that had seemed to her surely the tree of Praise. She had wanted at least one elm to be among the rising trees that would, at a future day, surround completely the forgotten factory, then advance within its fallen walls, not as a conquering army, but as a sheltering presence shading the wind-shattered glass, the bending steel, the crumbled urns, and the collapsing roof. Oak and maple would bring dignity to the trees' destined occupation of the space, but only the elm could speak some final praise for all that had been accomplished.

There had been times when Rachel had stood where she was standing now, looking out through the high casement windows, trying to *will* an elm into being. She would gaze at the slender sapling and, with near-painful concentration, try to force onto it the configurations and properties of the elm: the rough, layered bark, the oval leaf with the toothed edge, the green of the leaf somewhat pale as if there were a modesty, a humility, even in its praise.

But today, she had no power of concentration to give to the incipient elm; she had no appreciation of the afternoon light caught in the reflecting glass of the factory walls—the first kindling of an evening glow—or of the glint of gold given off by the rusting metal that framed the windowpanes. She could think only of her stupid brother, Peppy, and his million-dollar prank.

Again Rachel lifted the cup to her mouth. This time, when the lemon peel hit her upper lip she slurped it in and began to chew. Why had Peppy, who was not just her brother, but her *baby* brother, done such a thing? Never had she made known to him the Order's needs nor had she ever hinted at any particular want. Still, the money had come from Barbour, Tallent, Dempsey, and Hayes, beginning with two thousand sent a month after the fire at St. Michael's school, where Rachel had been principal. That Peppy had paid for the sanitarium and for the treatment Rachel had been given shortly after the fire, Rachel knew. But, in the light of this new evidence, she had to consider that that money too had been stolen.

No wonder her cure had been so strange: thievery had paid for it. Since her cure, she had often suspected that she would have been better off staying at the parish convent, in her room, until she could have pulled herself together. She'd been tired, that was all. She'd needed some rest, a good night's sleep, a few deep breaths. Instead of allowing herself to be carted off to an expensive hospital, she should have given her cheek a quick slap, straightened her spine, and squared her shoulders. Surely that would have shaken off the threatened madness. But she had failed to do so, and, to this day, this was a source not of guilt but of bafflement.

True, the treatment she'd been given had relieved her of her terror, but it had taken away her sense of certainty as well, the easy trust she'd had in herself and her judgments. Since the cure, as far as she could tell, she would *seem* to know, *seem* to understand, but she could seldom be sure. A possible answer was cause for further question. Did she *really* know? Did she *really* understand? The chance of error and misapprehension—suppressed or blithely discarded before her illness—was often present to her now. She would move among her perplexities like a troubled housekeeper searching for something misplaced, something needed or cherished, but now hidden from her. At times she would be exasperated with herself, at other times exasperated with what was lost, but more often she would simply keep herself alert, on the lookout for the old assurances, mourning their loss even as she begged for their return.

Exasperated now, she felt that if Peppy were there in the room with her, she'd give him a good swift knock on the side of the head. Because she loved him absolutely and beyond question, she had the right to hit him whenever she felt like it.

But these thoughts, in turn, made her see Peppy at age five, and herself at twelve. They were in the backyard of the house on Gedney Street. He was wearing his bib overalls with no shirt and no shoes, so it must be summer. She couldn't see what she herself was wearing except that the arm swinging out toward his head was bare. She could no longer remember what he'd done to deserve punishment, but that didn't matter. Her hand, palm open, landed on his skull, tipping his head away from her. His nose wrinkled upward and his eyes squinted in protest. He'd just had a hair cut, and the bone above the ear was almost bare. It was the memory of the bone and the shorn head that made Rachel uncurl her hand now. Had there been hair to hide the exposed skull, she might have wanted to hit him again but, as she remembered it now, he seemed so unprotected, all plucked and ugly, with almost no hair left. He seemed marked, an outcast. He had no protector, because he deserved none. He shouldn't have let his bones show. He shouldn't be so exposed, so shorn. Which was why she couldn't hit him, even now, knowing what she knew from the letter and the check in her pocket. With no one to protect him, she would become his protector. With no one to care because he was so ugly, she would care.

Again Rachel felt the great surge of protective love, fierce, defiant. She would defend her brother to the last shred of her own flesh. She would take to herself whatever might threaten him, there to do whatever evil it might choose to do, but not against her brother.

Rachel knew she should stop staring at the shoe factory. She knew from experience that, when she wanted to think a particular problem through to its solution, she should focus on something more manageable, less evocative. It should be an object that would suggest nothing beyond itself—if any such object existed. Something simple, not too intricate. Maybe a button on her smock would do. But no, the buttons were daubed with paint; the whole smock was splattered with all the colors she was using for her mural. The button would make her think of the painting, and the painting would lead her so far afield that her mind wouldn't come back for who knew how long.

She looked around the spacious room. A brass spindle on the foot of Mother's bed. No. Too close to Mother herself, to her illness, to her suffering. There was the huge fireplace, its carved and fluted columns suggesting a temple where a burning fire might be offered to the deity of the hearth. The grate was cold now, in May, but even in the freezing months a fire would be the last thing on which Rachel might try to focus her concentration.

Until Mother's illness there would have been Sister Angela's sewing machine to examine, or even the knobs and pulls on the TV set, but both had been taken downstairs to what had been the servants' sitting room. Because this had been the original owner's study, it had the one still-working bell device that connected with the pantry downstairs. With a press of the pearllike button in the alcove, a delicate "ping" would sound in the kitchen quarters below. Someone could then come, if not running, at least at a fairly brisk walk. Since Rachel was often in the refectory (no longer in use) painting her mural, she would hear the summons, quickly clean and wipe her hands, and come up to see what Mother wanted. What had been the convent's Common Room was now converted into the Mother General's sickroom, not because her status required so grand a chamber, but because the room had the last connection to the back of the house.

At first, at Mother's insistence, the sisters continued to gather there in the evenings, to sew, to read, to watch TV, to exchange gossip, or to do nothing at all. Mother had been grateful for the company. But when her condition worsened, all the communal artifacts—including Sister Martha's picture puzzle of the Brooklyn Bridge, still not finished—were taken away, leaving the room somber and emptied with little remaining but the old leather chairs, the bookcase, and the Mother General's narrow convent bed.

Rachel considered examining the books, but she'd already read all the titles, if not the books themselves—the Waverley novels of Scott, the complete works of Bulwer-Lytton and Thackeray, a stretch of shelf filled with Guizot's *History of France*, Strickland's *Lives of the Queens of England*. Oliver Wendell Holmes, Emerson, and James Russell Lowell, Carlyle and Ruskin—all by the yard—along with the ten volumes of *Lincoln, A History* by Nicolay and Hay. She'd also studied, more than several times, the spines, the pressed gold lettering, the often elaborate decorations that seemed Coptic in origin. The worn leather, the fading titles attracted her now, but she let her gaze wander to the wall opposite the window. There, above the dark oak paneling, rising almost to the ceiling, was a portrait of the man who had accumulated all these stately tomes, Mr. Timothy Flynn, the benefactor who had deeded the mansion to the Order, to the Sisters of the Annunciation.

Mr. Flynn was dressed in a tweedy brown suit with pants altered into knickers by his high laced boots. Perhaps some part of the portrait, some article of clothing, would provide Rachel with a particular point of mindless study so she could think without distraction. He had a reddish brown beard, a color the artist had reflected in the pink of his puffed-out cheeks and in the deeper red of his tiny up-tipped nose. He had almost no lips, but the lift of his cheeks suggested he was smiling. His eyes seemed dark gray; his forehead was high and untroubled; his hair less tawny than his beard and less curly. His right ankle was crossed in front of his left—which threatened to tilt the massive ovoid body off balance at any moment, especially since his hands were in his pockets and he'd have only his elbows to break the fall.

Because Mr. Flynn had flourished in an age when wealth was taken as a proof of God's favor—and God's favor was best exemplified by a well-fed corpulent body—the artist had done nothing to modify the fact that Timothy Flynn was fat. The body had a diameter rather than a waist; the sloping shoulders were a part of the general circumference; the arms, legs, and head were additions, embellishments to the spherical perfection of the torso itself. It was a telling commentary on the presentation of Mr.

Flynn that it had never been suggested that his portrait be removed from the Common Room. Never had he been considered a temptation; never had anyone thought that he might be a troublesome reminder of what the women had so willingly renounced. (On the contrary, he might well have suggested what they had been spared.)

Rachel considered studying the tip of Mr. Flynn's right boot—brown and slightly scuffed—but the way it touched the ground so lightly, so tentatively, made her sense the precarious balance of the body it sustained. She would look elsewhere. She then noticed that his trousers just below the left knee were beginning to look a little threadbare. The pocket, too, of his jacket was beginning to reveal signs of wear, a lighter brown showing through the dark tweed, and the weave of his lower left sleeve was slightly frayed. She looked again at the dusty boots. Mr. Flynn, it seemed, had not been idle in his gilded frame. It was as though he, too, had been laboring away, scuffing his boots and bringing his once splendid jacket to this shabby state, as if art itself offered no exemption from the consequence of daily toil.

It was of course time, not labor, that had worn through the expensive tweeds. Even to this lofty eminence above the dark paneling, the hours had reached and made their gentle rubbings of the boots, their slow, near-imperceptible loosening of the expert weave, the eventual rot of the sturdy thread.

It was as if Mr. Flynn, the revered benefactor, had chosen to follow the Order itself into poverty; that he had found this particular way to share its tattered fortunes and had asked no exemption from the general disintegration that had overtaken the object of his benefactions. He, no less than the sisters themselves, would submit not to the ravages of time, but to its caress, to the fond touch, the gentle graze that would wear away all that had seemed beyond the reach of years.

Yet he was somewhat less advanced in his disrepair. There he stood, still reasonably well-clothed, still robust, basically unaging except for one troubling blemish, a disturbing gray blotch just below the left eye. Given his present rate of dissolution, he would outlast by many years the imminent dispersal of the Order he had so generously endowed. Seven sisters remained of the once thriving community. With the death of the Mother General—which could come at any moment now—the remaining six were to be transferred to other Orders, other ministries, other missions, and even the great stone mansion that had been for them a sheltering parent, the Motherhouse, would be torn down to make way for the housing development that had long been approaching from the south and was poised even now just beyond the woods, impatient for the departure of the final nun.

If Mr. Flynn wanted to make his own disintegration concurrent with that of the Order, he would have to do better (or worse) than sport just a few worn threads and slightly marred boots. There would have to be nothing less than a savage rending of garments, a quick proliferation of the sickly gray blotch below the left eye. The boots would obviously never catch up; the tweeds would hold their weave for far too long. Well-intentioned Mr. Flynn might be willing to share with the Order even its demise, but the paint would never flake to dust in time for his own disappearance to coincide with the approaching dispersal. He would survive. That much was known. He was, eventually, to be removed to the state Historical Society, a donation by the Order after no buyer had been found even for the picture's frame. It would be in the gallery there, or in an attic or basement, that Mr. Flynn could continue his pursuit of the oblivion into which the Order would already have dissolved. Unnoted, his tweeds could coarsen and unravel, his boots take on the dust of many roads, and his face become increasingly disfigured by the already present blight.

Rachel was staring at the worn sleeve, trying to decide how she might apply her needle and make poor Mr. Flynn more presentable for his expulsion into the great world. It then occurred to her that this was a painting. It further occurred to her that she was a painter, that her days were given mostly to her mural of *The Last Supper* in the refectory downstairs. It then occurred to her that she—*she*—could patch his pants and jacket; she could bring back the shine to the boots. She might even find a cure for the threatened cheek. Slowly she reviewed her stock of

9

paints. She had the ochres, the yellows and greens and blacks with which to restore the tweeds; she could mix a brown to repair the boots; and she already knew she had the colors needed for a healthy flesh. Mr. Flynn should not go disgraced into public life. He would be in his prime, clothed and booted like the gentleman he had always been.

Rachel took another gulp of tea, but it tasted bitter. She drank it all the more quickly to get it over with. But she still hadn't made up her mind; she hadn't even begun to understand what her brother had actually done. She hadn't gotten beyond the knowledge that he was a thief and in jail. She did consider that that was all there was to know, but she wasn't ready yet to stop troubling herself, to give up the search for something less terrible, less wounding. She had yet to deal with the pride she felt for her brother, who had been so reckless on her behalf, on behalf of the Order. She had yet to feel the full anguish of his being imprisoned, shamed and reviled. She had yet to realize that all these irrefutable facts had anything to do with her brother, that this convicted felon *was* her brother.

Looking up at Mr. Flynn, it occurred to Rachel that a picture of Peppy, too, as a prime benefactor, should be hung up on the wall where time could slowly have its way and bring him to tatters and creeping death. Before she could repent of this appalling, forbidden thought, she heard a voice say, "You don't seem to use any yellow."

Mother was awake, but unmoving on the bed. Rachel, after the moment it took her to realize the meaning of the accusation, looked down at the smock she was wearing. It had been white to begin with, the kind a doctor wears to convince the patient he's antiseptic. Except that Rachel's smock was no longer white at all. Instead it came close to being a rather active abstract painting. Greens, browns, blues, reds, purples had been streaked, smudged, dabbed, splashed, or spattered onto the starched cloth. She had been trying to work on her painting, but the letter and the check had distracted her. Even though there was still an hour before she was supposed to give Mother her medicine, she'd fixed the tea and come upstairs anyway, hoping Mother would be awake.

Mother was awake now, but Rachel hadn't decided what to say to her. She kept her head lowered and continued to examine her smock. Mother had been right. There was almost no yellow. "Some of the figures have yellow hair," she said quietly.

"I don't mean on the painting. I mean on your smock. It's incomplete. More yellow. The upper right-hand corner. But not too much. Enough to bring out the blue." Mother raised her head a little. "Ah, and you've brought me some tea." A smile had lengthened Mother's mouth, giving her face the foolish look of someone whose expectations are founded on a misperception. Rachel looked down into the empty cup. She may have brought Mother some tea, but she'd just swallowed the last gulp herself. She'd even eaten the chunk of lemon.

"I hope you remembered to put in some lemon," Mother continued.

"Yes," Rachel said. "I remembered." Her voice was even quieter than before.

"Good. Without lemon, tea is so dingy. No wonder those English people put all that warm milk and sugar into it. All by itself, you might as well be drinking ditch water. Here. Help me sit up."

Rachel put the cup and saucer on the bedside table. She placed three pillows against the brass spindles of the headboard, then punched and plumped them. She put her arm under Mother's shoulders. "Ready?"

"I think so. Let's give it a try."

Mother bent her knees and drew her legs up under the blanket, then gave herself a shove backward. Rachel managed to lift the shoulders higher as Mother gave herself another push, both legs straightening as her body was moved up toward the brass bed frame. Rachel slid her hand up under Mother's head and brought it forward, out of the pillows.

"Is that better?" Rachel asked.

"I'm not sure. But let's just leave it." She was breathing heavily as if she'd just run up a flight of stairs.

"Would Mother like another pillow?"

"Just hand me the cup."

"Mother, I— I—"

"Just give it to me." Because Mother hadn't caught her breath, there was a desperation in her words. She began to cough.

Rachel took the cup and saucer from the bedside table and put them into Mother's trembling hands. Fortunately both saucer and cup were sturdy, thick white earthenware bought years ago from a diner that had closed during World War II. Mother started to bring them closer to her chin, but when she'd raised the cup halfway up the front of her nightclothes, she stopped. "Oh," she said. She was looking down into the cup. Before Rachel could explain, Mother said, "I've had my tea. I've already had it." She let out a small laugh from somewhere behind her nose, an attempt to diminish the seriousness of her mistake. "Of course. It was a little too hot, but by the time I'd eaten the lemon peel, it was just right."

The cup, as if it were about to tattle, began to clatter against the saucer. Mother's hand had begun to shake. "Here," she said, "Take it. I can't hold it anymore." As if in growing insistence that the truth be told, the cup rattled again and Rachel grabbed it just in time to keep it from toppling over the edge of the saucer. She steadied the cup, holding it firmly in her own hand.

"I drank the tea myself, while you were sleeping," Rachel said. She gave the cup a half turn in the ridges of the saucer, then put her hand over the top to hide the emptiness. "I ate the lemon too," she added. "And this morning—" She blurted out the words before she even knew she was saying them. "This morning I got a check for one hundred and eighty-seven dollars and thirty-two cents. It's really from my brother and he stole it. And he's in jail and—"

Before she could say anything more, Mother made a sudden jerk with her head and let out a quick gasp. Her body stiffened and she held her breath, trying not to make any sound. But the moan came out anyway, then a gasp, again trying to cut off whatever sound she might make. "Medicine. Quick."

Rachel put the cup and saucer back onto the bedside table. "Is it time? Did I forget?"

"You didn't forget. But it's time—" Mother arched her head backward as if trying to stretch it as far away from the rest of her body as she could. She raised her hands a few inches above the quilt and held them there. Her mouth quivered, but the words couldn't form themselves.

Rachel opened the drawer of the bedside table. There were the vials, the syringes, the needles. As if the scrape of the wood had calming powers, Rachel became patient and efficient. It was as though a tape recording had been turned on and she could hear the soft and careful voice of Mrs. Spinelli, the nurse who had trained Rachel in the care she was to give to Mother. Obeying instructions as if they were being spoken aloud, Rachel picked up one of the packets containing a sterile swab, tore it open, and extracted the small swatch of gauze. It felt cold against her fingers. Next she took one of the vials, pried off the small metal cap and rubbed the swab against the rubber stopper.

"Tell me again, what you were saying," Mother gasped. "Quick. Don't stop. Stolen, you said. Quick—a check, you said. How much—?"

Calmly, carefully, Rachel pulled away the plastic cover protecting the needle and inserted the needle through the stopper, into the clear liquid inside the vial. "It doesn't matter," she said. "It doesn't matter."

"It matters. Tell me— How—"

Rachel lifted the blanket, gently, not hurrying, and even more gently raised the side of Mother's flannel nightgown. "One hundred eighty-seven dollars and thirty-two cents." She rubbed a fresh swab against Mother's thigh, examined the syringe to make sure the fluid was at the needle's mouth, then stuck the needle into a pinch of muscle. With her thumb she pressed the plunger, forcing the fluid through.

"He stole one hundred eighty-seven dollars—" Mother gasped the words out two at a time. "And they put him in jail? For that?"

"He's in jail for stealing twenty-three thousand. Four years, the letter said."

"Twenty-three thousand? That's more—more like it."

After she'd withdrawn the needle, Rachel blotted the skin where the puncture had been made, more a gesture of apology than a medical

13

necessity. "But he stole more. Much more." She straightened the nightgown and brought the blanket back up.

Mother let her outstretched arm fall limply onto the quilt. She had closed her eyes as if she didn't want to be present for her own pain. She was panting, her shoulders rising and falling, unable to slow down. She pushed her head farther back into the pillows. "I wasn't going to take the medicine, not anymore—" Her words came out one breath at a time, the voice still hoarse. "Identify myself with those in pain and there's no help for them. Let my own come I said. Let it come—"

"Mother should try to rest now—"

"I am resting. See me? Lying here? I'm resting."

"Then maybe you should try to sleep."

"I did sleep. I just woke up. You were here. You saw me. I'm not ready to sleep. Not yet. I want to hear more about—about—brother. But wait. I was going to refuse the medicine. Mortification. Accept. So many people, suffering. Be with them. Like them. Feel what they feel." She shook her head slowly. "But no. I won't. I will not accept it!" She pulled in a quick breath and let it come out through her nose, a snorted laugh. "Too much in the world already. Everywhere. It's enough. Too much!"

She pulled in another breath and swallowed it, gulping down the air. Again she shook her head. "Let there be less, then I'll do my share. Gladly. Become a dope fiend—what do I care? No pain, if it can be helped. None. I refuse! End *theirs*, then I'll accept mine. Take away their suffering and I'll welcome mine. But no; they are in pain—enough. I refuse! End theirs, then bring me mine. Not until then!" With rapid jerks of her head she seemed to be trying to shake off the words even as she said them, trying to rid herself of the ideas even as she thought them.

"Would Mother like another—I mean, more of the medicine?"

The jerking slowed, then stopped. Mother's breathing was even, but still difficult, her chest heaving. "No," she whispered. "Just keep talking to me. . . . Tell me more. Your brother. I want to hear. Please. A fine story. A good story. Thief. And your brother. Jail. Good. More. Tell me more."

"I wasn't going to say anything."

"But you did. And now you've got to go on. It sounded... distracting. Distract me. Let me hear it. All of it...."

Slowly Rachel reached into the pocket of her smock and picked out the half-crumpled envelope. "A check," she said. "And a letter." She pulled out the papers.

"Good. Yes, a letter too. Good."

The check slid from between the folds of the letter and floated in waltz time to the floor. "The check, it's really from my brother."

"Brother. Yes. The one in jail."

"The money—even the check—it's all embezzled."

"Oh?"

"Yes. Twenty-three thousand. At least that's what they said in court. I mean, that's what the letter said they said in court. And now, this check, the letter says it closes out his special account."

Mother's breathing came slower now. She nodded again a few times. "I see your brother waited until his fortunes were somewhat depleted before he managed to think of us."

"No. Not really," Rachel said softly. "I think it was my brother who gave us the money for the library at the college. Money he stole. And the donation so we didn't have to close St. Brigid's for two more years. I think he stole that too. And... and I don't know what else. And...."

"Him? Your brother?"

"If Mother will look at the letter—it's signed by the same lawyer, a Mr. Thomas Tallent. It's from the same company, the same firm. Look. Barbour, Tallent, Dempsey, and—"

"—and Hayes? Barbour, Tallent, Dempsey, and Hayes? The blessed four? They've been representing your brother?"

"It would seem so."

"And what is his name? Your brother's name?"

"Peppy."

"Peppy? That's not a brother. That's a dog."

"Phillip. His name is Phillip. We called him Peppy. Like I was Aggie.

And our brother George, he was Porgie. Like in Georgie Porgie, Puddin' and Pie. But Phillip. It...it's really Phillip."

"Well, I should hope so. Is he the preternaturally handsome one who used to come visit you, a long time ago, in the hospital? Corn-colored hair, brown eyes. Everyone all atwitter? Even one of the doctors?"

"Yes, brown eyes. Hair, yes. Peppy. I mean, Phillip."

"Inordinately presentable if I remember."

"People seem to think so."

"And you?"

"Me? Oh. Yes. Yes, I do."

"Then it's for Phillip Manrahan that we pray when we give our thanks for all that help? For your brother, Peppy? Imagine. All those prayers, all those blessings. For Peppy Manrahan."

"But no. The real people who gave the money, they're the company he worked for. It was their money, not his. The company's. Olympix, with an x at the end."

"Olympix? You mean all these years we've been calling down uncounted blessings on something called Olympix?"

"It's the name of the company he...he..."

"Stole from."

"Yes. Stole from."

"Well, it would seem to me he should get part of the credit. He must have worked at it very hard. You don't embezzle more than a million without applying yourself. He must be very gifted, your Peppy."

"He's a genius."

"Well, not quite. Or at least not genius enough. He *is* in jail, don't forget."

"But only for twenty-three thousand."

"Ah, how jaded we've become with our talk of a million. Twenty-three thousand is as nothing to us, is it?"

"It's all they could prove. They hinted at the trial, the letter says, that there was a lot more, but they couldn't find it."

"Of course they couldn't find it. *We* had it." Mother laughed, then coughed out the words. "What a wonderful man your Peppy is. I shall pray for him and he shall be showered with such blessings. And never— never—will I breathe in prayer the pagan name Olympix. Let them fend for themselves."

"But the money really belongs to them. Shouldn't they know what they've given? And to whom?"

"And land your brother in jail for another thousand years? Is that what you want?"

"I want—I want—oh, Mother, please—what am I supposed to want?"

Mother looked long at Rachel, then patted the quilt next to her. "Come, Sister. Sit here by me. I'm better now. It's all going away, the pain. Hold my hand. Here." Again she patted the quilt.

"But what am I—"

"Ssssh. No more talk about brothers and checks and prisons and letters. Let's just think of nothing for a while. Hold my hand and we'll think of absolutely nothing. It's another way of prayer. To do nothing, to think nothing, to be nothing. A complete surrender. Come, Sister. Together we shall become nothing but God's, and he will smile on us, and we won't even bother to know that we are being blessed."

After Mother had given the quilt another succession of pats, Rachel sat down on the bed. Mother pressed Rachel's hand in both of her own, holding it in tender captivity as if trying to catch its throb and pulse. Then she brought it slightly toward her and let it rest, still gently held, on the wide band of white sheet folded down over the top of the quilt. Slowly with Mother's breathing, the held hands rose and fell, rising and falling, a small barque on a quiet sea. "Now we are nothing," Mother whispered.

Rachel begged that she be nothing, that she know nothing, that she do nothing. But it did no good. It was Olympix's money. It was Olympix's library wing, Olympix's roofs, Olympix's plaster and paint, Olympix's computers—even though they might have some difficulty retrieving any of it since it was now all in the hands of the Order's creditors. But shouldn't Olympix at least get a tax break?

17

She looked down at Mother's hands holding her own. They were already skeletal, the knuckles stretching the skin to what must be the point of pain, the tendons thick beneath the taut flesh, the tracery of veins a milky white. Her breathing had slowed even more, but it held itself to a rhythm of rise and fall, at an ease now that seemed beyond contentment. On her eyelids the veins were blue as if they were draining away the blue of her once fierce eyes. Her face, too, could no longer hide the death mask waiting to reveal itself, the broad forehead, the hollowing eye sockets, the sunken cheeks, the stretched mouth, the fallen chin. Yet, there on the chin were three dark hairs sprouting from a mole, the mole itself a small mound of tiny brown specks bubbling up from the skin, an attempt to escape in time from the dying flesh. This was Sister Gabriel, the Mother General, the woman who had been Head of Novices when Agnes Manrahan, soon to become Sister Mary Rachel of the Sisters of the Annunciation, had first entered the Order more than forty years before, at the age of seventeen. Rachel had forgotten that she loved her, but she remembered now.

From across the room, near the fireplace, came a creak of the old floorboards. The brush of the bedsheet against itself as Mother breathed in and out, up and down, sounded like low suspirations as if the bed, too, were breathing along with the two silent women. Somewhere below them, in another part of the great house, a door closed with a slight squeal of surprise, and from the highway half a mile away came the high whine of speeding cars. The door opened again, then closed, a bird, a thrush maybe, trilled in a distant tree, the floorboards creaked again, this time from somewhere near the windows. Motes sifted in a shaft of sunshine, each vying with the other for a place in the light. The letter Rachel had jammed back into her pocket crinkled a little, then stopped.

It was only when some high-pitched laughter—two girls it must be, or three—was heard from beneath the windows that Rachel raised her head. The laughter came again, the girls going no doubt from the housing development to the river or to the pear orchard. The laughter repeated itself, only this time more prolonged, with one girl outlasting the others. Mother had opened her eyes and was waiting, listening for more. Rachel didn't move, but when the laughter became more distant, she looked down at the quilt, drew her hand slowly toward herself, and put it back into her pocket.

Mother splayed her fingers across her eyes, even though the afternoon light could hardly have bothered them. "They sounded like postulants." She repeated the word: "postulants," the designation given to those just entering the Order. She seemed to savor the word, as if it suggested a distant country visited long ago and almost forgotten. Then she, too, laughed. And coughed. "How great was my despair in those days. So many of them. What were we going to do with them? How were we going to care for so many? How were we going to teach them, pray for them, bless them? Where would we send them? New schools must be started, new missions must be founded. Otherwise there'd be nothing for them to do. Their calling would be lost, wasted. Some way must be found. But so many of them."

From the distance the laughter came again. "Go see who it is," Mother said. "Out the window, look. See who they are." She took her fingers away from her eyes and held up her hand, palm outward. "Quick."

Rachel got up from the bed and went to the window. It was already open, but because of the screen, she couldn't lean out. Still, with the edge of her eye, she saw—or thought she saw—the last twirl of a skirt disappearing around the corner of the house. The skirt was red and of thicker material than one would have expected on a spring day. Because Rachel wasn't quite sure she'd seen it, she pressed her nose against the screen, but it was too late. The skirt had definitely disappeared—if it had been there to begin with.

Since her cure, Rachel had sometimes thought she'd seen, from the corner of her eye, before she could look directly at it for verification, the bright colors of a robe or a skirt, disappearing out a door or around a corner. It was as if she had come moments too late for an appointment, that some messenger, weary of waiting, had finally given up and left just as Rachel had arrived. She would sometimes call out, but it never helped. Whoever it might have been was already gone. A look through a door, around a corner, into the next room, revealed no one.

Of course it was a trick of the eye. Some particle of dust, brilliantly colored, but dust nevertheless, that had come into her peripheral vision and become magnified for just that single moment before passing on. It was one more instance of the general disorientation brought on by her treatment, her cure. It was either a trick of the eye or a trick of the brain, or the two in collusion. Together, her eye and her brain would conspire to create this momentary vision. It had a physical source, a medical explanation. If she had told Dr. Zaug about it, he would solemnly lay before her in patient detail a complete and convincing diagnosis of the phenomenon. He would reassure her; he would try to calm her perplexity; he would dismiss the vision itself.

Which is why Rachel never mentioned it to Dr. Zaug, or to anyone. She was ashamed of having seen it. It had been the Angel of the Annunciation. The bright colors, the rich and vanishing robes, told her that. It was not an optical tease, no matter what she might tell herself. It was not the projection of a corrected brain. It was a messenger come with some pronouncement that would restore Rachel to herself. All the memories of which she had been robbed would be returned to her and take up their rightful places in her mind. Her old certainties would be newly sustained. All bewilderment would be banished, and she would be made whole again.

That the messenger had always eluded her, that the message itself remained unspoken, was a sorrow to her, but someday she would arrive on time. She would find herself in the heavenly presence. With uplifted wings, not of feathers but of golden leaves, the Angel, robed in splendid brocades of red shot through with threads of gold, would speak the needed words, and Rachel, too awed, too joyful to bow down, would receive the awaited message. And—the true miracle of it all—she would *understand* what had been said. It was for this understanding that she waited. For this she begged, for this she lived in constant expectation, in humility and in hope.

But the quick rush of the red skirt had passed out of her sight, around the side of the mansion. For once it could not have been a trick of the eye. Or of the mind. It had been the red skirt of the laughing girl who was, at this moment, passing under the porte cochere, going toward the orchard.

Mother, her hand still held up and outward, let out a long breath, closer to a groan than a sigh. "They're gone. I thought maybe they'd like to come in, to visit. Maybe they'd like to see the house. It's a beautiful house. We could give them cocoa. And they could tell us . . . tell us about their lives, the way the new girls, the postulants always did, about movie stars and singers we'd never heard of, and about so much that's new in the world. We'd hear about fathers and mothers and brothers and sisters; they'd tell us their names. All the names of all the people we'd never know about if they hadn't come to tell us. And I—you—both of us— we'd tell them—we—you—I—" She stopped and lowered her hand. "You can come away from the window. They're gone." Her voice was flat, without inflection, and Rachel felt the failure had been hers.

She stepped back from the window. Waiting for further instruction, she stood there, looking through the screen toward the wide river. No boats moved on the water, and the traffic bridge off to the south that looked like it had been made from her brother George's Erector Set had so few cars that she could count them. Four coming west, toward her, seven going east, away from her. One was red.

Rachel went to the side of the bed. "Would Mother like to sleep now, or should I get you something first?"

"Nothing. I'll sleep now. But you might want to wash your face. What'd you do to your nose?"

Rachel reached up and touched her nose. "Nothing," she said.

"It's all black. On the tip."

"Oh. The screen." She rubbed her sleeve against her nose, looked at the sleeve, then rubbed her nose again. "Clean?"

"Reasonably."

"I'll come back in a little while. If you want anything—"

"I won't. Go finish your painting. It's certainly taking you long enough."

"It's a very big wall."

"You could have picked the smaller one. The one at the far end."

"I need the big one."

"You and Leonardo, both so fussy. When he did his *Last Supper,* it couldn't have taken this long."

"He had helpers."

"Well, get yourself some."

"No. Nobody can see until it's finished."

"Temperament. But go ahead. Only use a little more yellow. Not necessarily on the painting, but at least on your smock."

"I'll try."

"All right, all right. Go on. Sometimes I get the feeling I won't die until that painting of yours is finished."

"I would like Mother to see it. When it's finished."

"All right. I won't die then, until it's all painted."

Rachel went to the door. "Would Mother like me to hurry? With the painting?"

There was no answer at first. Then Mother said, "Yes. If you don't mind."

Before Rachel could close the door behind her, she heard Mother say, "Oh—and about the money, about your brother, this preternaturally handsome Peppy, I would suggest—no, I think I'd better command—under the vow of obedience—I command you to keep your trap shut. Understood? Nothing to Messrs. Barbour, Tallent, Dempsey, and what's his name. Spend the money you got on paint—and forget the rest. Understand?"

"Yes, Mother."

"And you may, if you want, write to your brother and thank him for the check sent in his name. But no mention of the others."

"But shouldn't I warn him? Shouldn't I 'admonish' him?"

"Warn him of what?"

"Well, he could go to hell. I mean, he *is* a thief. And he's never sorry about what he does. I know him. He's never sorry. He could go to hell."

"Oh. That. Well, that's the chance one takes."

Mother closed her eyes. Rachel backed out the door.

TWO

Phillip set the violin onto his collarbone, then lowered his jaw onto the chin rest. It didn't feel comfortable. And he didn't have a clean handkerchief to cushion the plastic. He looked around his cell. His washcloth was wet. A pair of jockey shorts would have lumpy seams. A sock would work, but there, too, none was clean. A dirty one would have to do. He searched among the rumpled clothes stuffed into a plastic shopping bag and found a green cotton sock that wouldn't scratch. He gave it a quick whiff. It was rather pleasing in its own sweaty way. He folded it, placed it over the chin rest and again lowered his jaw. The fit was perfect and the odor somewhat comforting, a reassurance that his body was still giving off the usual roseate smells.

He was in need of the consolation. On his bunk lay a letter from his sister Aggie—also known as Sister Mary Rachel of the Sisters of the Annunciation. The letter distressed him. She knew he was in prison; she knew he had been convicted of embezzlement. She might also know that the check sent to her had come from the same firm that had represented the anonymous donor whose benefactions had sustained her Order for more than several years.

It was Phillip's first hope that his sister would fail to make the connection. He would hardly want her to know that he'd stolen slightly more than a million dollars. But it was his second hope that she *would* make the connection. He had wanted, of course, to protect her from any knowledge of his malefactions, of his embezzlements. But he had wanted, at moments, for his sister to know that he had taken risks on her behalf. Even more, he had wanted to suggest that he was making atonement for what he had done to her. He had robbed her of herself. It was he, with his first embezzlements, who had paid for the treatments that had relieved her of her suffering, but the treatments had relieved her of herself as well. They had removed her from the woman she'd been and placed her at a distance where she would be safe, where she would be protected from the grief that had maddened her in the first place. But she was no longer Aggie. She was the repository of Aggie. Aggie dwelt somewhere within her, unable to emerge, unable to return from the distant country to which he'd sent her.

At times Phillip wanted nothing so desperately as to rescue her, to release her from the gentle prison to which she'd been committed. But then he would would see the suffering that such a freedom might inflict on her again: the old horror would be unleashed, the tamed grief reawakened and perhaps, the madness come again. He would take no chances. She must stay as she was. The letter from the lawyers—and the check—must mean nothing extraordinary to her. It was his prayer that she never make the connection. And, from the simple contents of her letter, he encouraged himself to believe his prayer might have been answered. She had limited herself to thanks for the check. She would pray for him. And when the Mother General no longer needed her care, she would come to visit him.

Long life to the Mother General was his second prayer.

Phillip lowered the violin bow. Four good D-naturals—a most rare beginning for a fugue—then moving downward to a B-flat, the first voice finely sounded. Quickly he moved through the tonic chord, the

G-minor triad that gave the sonata its name. Maybe now he could stop thinking about the letter, about his sister. Now the second voice of the fugue, the answer, starting not on G but moving on to F then E-flat, then eventually to G. O rare Johann Sebastian, O cunning Johann Sebastian, O glorious Johann Sebastian Bach.

"If you can play the Bach G-*Minor*," his grandfather had said, "you can play anything." Phillip could not play the G-*Minor*, nor would he ever, not really. But he could work at it. There had even been, over the years, some days when it seemed he was on the brink of discovery, that the inner workings—apparent only to the true artist—might surface, they would reveal themselves, he would know them and pounce on them. But just as the moment was about to arrive, the sonata's deeper secrets would—out of modesty?—hide themselves again from his all-too-eager opportunings.

Still, the coaxing had continued, and would continue for the rest of his life. In between, as respite, he could still play the *Kreisler Etudes* that had been his first real achievements. He could also saw his way through the violin part of Beethoven's *Kreutzer* and scrape together a rondo here and there. But then, eventually, he would have to return to the Bach, to the G-*Minor*.

Phillip's first lessons had been not at his grandfather's knee, but at his elbow. He had always been attracted to the violin because it had a peculiar shape, it was shiny, it made noise, and because he was forbidden to touch it or even go near it. He was indifferent to his grandfather's playing until when he was about seven, the music had become more and more scratchy, more dissonant, and decidedly slower. His grandfather's arthritis was asserting itself. One night, after Nathan Millstein had played on the Bell Telephone Hour, the fugue from the Bach sonata, his grandfather took the violin out of the dining room cupboard and began to play—not the fugue, but the opening adagio. All the notes were wrong. None led to the other. But his grandfather persisted. The huge freckles on his forehead, great brown blotches like splats of dirty rain-water, stood out more than usual. His lips were thrust forward, his nostrils stiffened and wide. Then he stopped, but held the bow in position.

Without thinking of how stupid his question was, Phillip had said, "Would you like me to help?"

It was then that his lessons began.

The intoxication Phillip always found when playing the fugue was already beginning: the several voices, singular, insistent on themselves, yet being sounded together in such incredible harmony. Why couldn't it have been Bach who'd created the world? (Or had he?) Now the yearning began, the need, growing more and more desperate, to hear the G-minor tonic. It was pressing him, forcing him onward.

But then his nerves began their usual, inevitable hum. Up ahead were the triple stops just after the second exposition, a passage of consecutive eighth notes, which his grandfather had rightly dubbed "a real knuckle-breaker." But this time he'd make it. He was determined.

He didn't, of course, make it. He had to stop; he had to start again— at the beginning of the second exposition, almost as if this were the way Bach had written it: with a start, a stop, another start, another stop, a repeated passage of consecutive eighth notes meant to madden and humble even the best—and to remind Phillip that he was far, far from the best.

On the third try, he *thought* he might have made it, but didn't examine too closely what he'd heard. And at least no one else had heard either. For a change, his mistakes, his wrathful second and third attempts were heard only by himself. Prison was the perfect place in which to play the violin. In the apartment he'd lived in before being able to buy a house, he had always to expect Mrs. Toohey's elephantine foot pounding on the ceiling or Cory Zarzicki's fist banging on the wall, but here, in jail, he could fiddle away and no one cared. He could fiddle in the morning, fiddle in the evening, and fiddle in the summertime. His cell, a room actually, rather like one in a somewhat severe college dorm—a model experiment in penal reform—had apparently been built with his violin in mind. Concrete above and below, concrete to the right of him, concrete to the left, with a window no more than six inches wide, but reaching almost from floor to ceiling. Opposite the window was an impregnable door with a square foot of double glass set into it, a distraction for the guard who might have nothing better to do than observe his charges at work and at play. The state authorities, in their charity and compassion, had given Phillip the room he'd been wanting for years.

Also, there would be hours and hours during which he could practice. Obedient to the passage in Ecclesiastes, he had a set schedule, a time for getting up and a time to go to bed, a time for work and a time for play, a time to eat and a time to read, a time to walk and a time to sit, a time to talk and a time to shut up, a time to be locked in and a time to be let out. He liked the orderliness of it all. If he had any complaints, it was that not enough time was allowed for work. It began at eight-thirty and was all over at three-thirty. With lockup and head-count at four o'clock, there was no chance of putting in overtime. He considered it a disruption to be told he had to stop at three-thirty sharp.

Phillip was being taught tailoring, his choice among several possibilities, when butcher, baker, and candlestick maker were not available. Since it was assumed (rightly) that his days as a money manipulator, an accountant, were at an end, it was hoped that an ability to sew would rescue him from a life of crime. Where he would find a job making uniforms for those in maximum-security prisons—as he was doing now—remained a mystery. He had never seen such a job listed in the want ads, but no doubt the authorities knew more about it than he did.

When he'd worked as an accountant, however, he'd been allowed to stick around and juggle his figures for as long as he'd wanted. No one seemed to mind when he'd stay in the office until nine o'clock or sometimes midnight.

It wasn't ambition that had kept him there; it was, in the beginning at least, his fascination with numbers. He was endlessly intrigued by their strict, immutable quality, yet also by the way in which they could be placed in near-infinite combinations. Rather like musical notes, relationships could be shifted, manipulated. A number was a perfect slave. It was unchanging in itself, it was known in its entirety, it had no ambition to be other than itself, but it was ever at the service of anyone smart enough to give it instruction.

The earliest intimation of Phillip's mastery over numbers came when, to please his superiors, he had managed to organize the figures in such a way that fees and collections increased while taxes and tariffs diminished. But never was his talent praised. The corporation found it sufficient to reward his "competence" by not promoting him to a position that would remove him from the numbers and figures he had so effectively subdued.

Phillip made no complaint. His indignation—a cold, barely repressed fury that would happily have expressed itself in mayhem—was given another more productive outlet. When word came to him that his sister, Aggie, had suffered some sort of emotional collapse, his excursions into the company coffers began. Both his rage at the corporation and his concern for his sister could now be accommodated by a single act: embezzlement. Then, without pause, Phillip decided that his experience in dispensing largesse needn't end with his sister's release from the hospital. He could rob at random and the resulting plunder funneled to the Sisters of the Annunciation. Phillip had congratulated himself for the simplicity of the arrangement and thanked the Fates in general for their cooperation in providing him with this most gleeful form of revenge against the indifferent, unappreciative Olympix.

Phillip's prison sentence, fortunately, was for only the amount stolen when an office colleague, Jack Sandy, came down with AIDS. Jack needed money. With the corporation's complicity, Jack's insurance had been canceled. Phillip was enraged, as he was often enraged. Unknown to almost everyone, he had something of a monumental temper. And, as usual, he deflected it by a quick switch onto another track. Instead of ranting against the corporation and the insurance company, instead of denouncing them and having a fit complete with thrown objects and a smashing of things, he reverted to his previous form of sublimated frustration: embezzlement. He'd long since stopped his thieveries, but

Sandy's predicament required their renewal. His sister's Order had been in a state of dissolution for over three years; it no longer required the exercise of his talents. But with the cutoff of his friend's health care, he felt the old stirrings and had hesitated not at all. He told Jack he knew where he might get some money, from an anonymous source. Jack blessed him and the source, but lived to need only twenty-three thousand.

Phillip was arrested two days after the funeral and shrugged off any questions about where the money might have gone. He had not been careless about this latest theft. Some computer hacker, just out of school, was exploring the full range of the corporation's worldwide reach—just for his own illegal amusement—when he unearthed a few bewildering figures. This excited him to new illegalities, new searches, new checks and balances—and the rest took care of itself. And of Phillip too.

Phillip had reached the repeated D's on the downbeat—the excitement of hitting the open string, then hitting it again and again and again—the tension, the expectation intensifying with each stroke.

G-minor *had* to be sounded, the full chord, the complete gathering, the final fulfillment of all he had been tending toward. But not yet, not yet. Keeping Mr. Bach's measured pace, he found himself begging for it, for the G-minor proclamation, but all he was given was delay, delay, exquisite delay—one incredible, almost inhuman incitement after another. The G-minor conclusion—cadence, climax, fulfillment—was there, up ahead, but not yet, not yet. Phillip had to wonder how many listeners knew how sexually explicit Bach could be.

At first, Phillip heard the knock on the door as a rap of his knuckle against the belly of the violin, even though he knew it couldn't be. When it came again, with its own intrusive rhythm, he heard it as a disruption of his thrust toward the G-minor cadence, a deliberate attempt to deny him the release toward which he'd been so ardently striving. When the knock came again, with the G-minor still unfulfilled, but coming closer, he found himself—against all principle—looking toward the door.

There, through the glass, he saw the face of a young man from his tailoring class, the inmate who claimed for himself the improbable name of Talford Starbuck. His eyes were wide with some kind of expectation and he was waving, like a wayward metronome, what looked like a Milky Way candy bar. Phillip tried to keep right on playing. The young man gave the Milky Way a few more waves, then lowered it beneath the frame of the glass. He continued to look in, his eyes less wide now beneath the pressure of a wrinkling forehead. His mouth was slightly open, and he blinked twice, then again, as if he hoped what he was seeing might change between blinks.

Phillip remembered him only too well. Talford Starbuck was his self-appointed mentor. Since the tailoring classes were, to say the least, fluid, with new recruits arriving haphazardly, at the whim of the criminal justice system rather than at the beginning of a set semester, it was left to those further along to help those who'd newly arrived. Mr. Starbuck, who seemed to consider himself more instructor than pupil, spent most of the sessions moving freely among the untutored, Phillip included. Explaining, correcting, cajoling, all with the sure, somewhat prissy authority of a school matron. (It had surprised Phillip to discover that his tutor had begun his five-year sentence for breaking-and-entering only three days before Phillip's own enrollment.)

Phillip yanked the bow up, away from the violin. "What do you want?" he yelled. The young man leaned his face closer to the window, touching it with the tip of his nose as if he might be able to hear, Helen Keller fashion, from the vibrations of the glass. He opened his mouth but didn't form any words.

"What do you—?" Phillip knew it wouldn't do any good to keep asking the same question over and over again. The only way to end the intrusion was to find out what it was all about, dismiss it, then take up again his thrust toward G-minor. He undid the lock, and Talford Starbuck himself turned the knob and pulled the door open. Phillip stood in the doorway, offering no greeting, only the expectation that the young man had something to say, and it had better be urgent. But the young man said nothing. He just stayed where he was, looking up at Phillip.

A head shorter than Phillip, Talford Starbuck had a baby face and wispy blond hair. Although he had a well-formed body, the upward tilt of his snub nose made his nostrils a fairly compelling feature, suggesting—if one were sufficiently uncharitable—the snout of a baby pig. It had once occurred to Phillip during class, when Talford was showing him how to thread his bobbin, that the young man must have reached the peak of his perfection at about six months of age and had then pretty much stopped his development, retaining all his infant features under the impression that this would assure him a lifetime of ogles and squeezes. Then, when the pokes and pinches stopped, the boy had apparently continued his expectations, more puzzled than disappointed when they were not forthcoming, but still persisting in the expectation.

"You want something?" Phillip asked.

Starbuck organized his lips into a half-smile. "You were playing the violin." He seemed proud of the insight.

"Yes. I know."

The young man held out the candy bar, still smiling. "I brought you something."

Phillip pulled back. "Oh?"

"It's for you."

"I don't get it."

"I saw you eating one once."

"I'm sorry, but I think there's been a mistake."

"No. It's yours."

Wary but interested, Phillip took the Milky Way from Starbuck's outstretched hand. Immediately, the young man's eyes widened, his ears pulled back a little, and his hairline rose. He took a step inside the room. The door closed behind him as if pushed by an unseen hand.

Phillip was completely amazed. This was an impermissible presumption. The young man had actually come into his room, just stepped inside without invitation or request as if responding to a God-given right. Whether Phillip should be affronted, amused, or aghast, he wasn't sure. He looked down at the candy bar, then again at Starbuck. "Now that I've taken it, is there anything else you'd like me to do?"

"Aren't you going to eat it?"

"I might. Why? You want to watch?"

"Oh no. I just meant that's why I gave it to you. So you could eat it."

"I'll do that. Anything else?"

"You don't want me to sit down or anything?"

"Not particularly."

"Oh?"

"I was playing my violin. As you so rightly observed."

Starbuck glanced back at the door, then tried to look directly at Phillip, but seemed unable, as if Phillip's face were something he'd been warned not to look upon. Finally, he settled for the third button down on Phillip's shirt. "You don't want me to listen?"

"I was just practicing. It wouldn't be anything worth hearing."

"I could listen anyway. If you want me to."

To be as polite as possible, Phillip was about to suggest some other time when, over Starbuck's shoulder, he saw the face of Roger Butte in the door window. The face moved to the left, giving half the window to Jason Folger. Butte and Folger—Phillip was on a last-name basis with all the prisoners, even in his mind—were the two most famous inmates on the tier. Together, they led a small and merry band that pretty much dominated cellblock D, not by force or fear, but by energy. Wherever they might be, Butte, Folger, and their followers took the place over by an excess of enthusiasm. In the gym, they managed to possess the basketball court by means of superior enjoyment; the workout equipment, the weights, and the machines were appropriated by their joyful demonstrations of how it should all be done; the TV room was commandeered because no one felt he could compete with the obvious pleasure they got from what they wanted to see. In the yard they ignored the handball and tennis courts, but were generally unchallenged in their claim to the baseball diamond. They seemed to establish their rights not by bullying or by threats, but by an appreciation no one else could equal.

They were not the druggies, the dealers, the needle people who formed a great part of the prison population. They were neither resentful nor contemptuous; they didn't snarl, neither did they sneer. Violence was beyond their consideration, rebellion unthinkable. They were different from everyone else—and great amounts of energy were spent in the proof of it.

It was, of course, a conspiracy. To the authorities, the guards, the counselors, the various boards and committees, Butte, Folger, and the others refused to present themselves as sullen and defeated criminals; they were determined to enjoy—or pretend to enjoy—the life provided them. Any expectation of remorse was destined for disappointment. Any demand for a show of guilt was joyfully mocked, any hope for even minimal penitence would be frustrated by an ebullient response to a command, the cheerful performance of a task, or the buoyant participation in the fun and games encouraged by the state.

Butte and Folger were all the authorities could hope for—and then some. Who could fault their behavior? No therapist, no board member, no committee chair, no warden, no guard. And so the staff members retreated into the only response available to them: the wary patience of the mocked, the taut vigilance of the ridiculed, sustained mostly by the certainty that the energy would someday have to flag, since good cheer was not an easy emotion to maintain, and enthusiasm was not famous for its durability. Someday surely the energy would be beaten back into sullenness and the enthusiasms reduced to a sulk. But until then, the merry band presented to all but the keenest eye the appearance of a peaceable kingdom presided over by a benevolent staff and peopled by citizens of uncommon good will.

Butte and Folger remained unmoving in the window, each allowing the other a one-eyed view of what was inside. An outcropping from Folger's overgrown crew cut had thrust itself in among the massed curls on Butte's head, and their flesh seemed joined at the temple and along the line of the cheek. Because Folger had the larger, longer nose, he gave the composite face its main feature, although Butte's dark brown eye made a not unworthy contribution, especially compared to the hazel-green provided by Folger. Folger, however, brought to their union by far the more seemly mouth, the better-shaped jaw, and it was to Butte's advantage that his scraggly moustache and receding chin had been partly forced off the right side of the frame and he was able, for the moment, to claim some part of the firm, forward jaw of his friend, Folger.

"Is that Butte behind me, at the door?" Starbuck asked. He shifted his eyes, as if hoping he might be able to see through the back of his head.

"Butte and Folger. Two for the price of one."

Starbuck winced. "I knew Butte was after me, but I guess he wants Folger to point for him."

"Point?"

"Point. You know what point means."

Philip knew what, in prison jargon, "point" meant, but this was becoming a conversation he'd prefer not to have, especially with Talford Starbuck. "Aim your finger in a particular direction? Lift your front paw and stick out your tail?"

"It means watch out if somebody's coming. Be a lookout. Point. How can you not know that?" Starbuck seemed more frightened than surprised by Phillip's ignorance.

"I have a lot of things I don't know. I like it that way."

"Are they still there?"

"There's more of Folger than Butte, but, yes, they're still there."

"What are they doing?"

"Looking at the back of your head and the front of mine."

"Tell them to go away."

"Why? Anybody's welcome to look any time he wants to."

This was far from the truth, but he wanted to lightly punish the poor young man for being so serious. It had occurred to Phillip that Starbuck had gotten it into his head that Butte and Folger were—God save them!—interested in him, that they wanted to spirit him off to some dark corner and have their way with him. Here, no doubt, was yet another proof that a lack of intelligence leaves far too much room for the imagination. Neither Butte nor Folger could conceivably be interested in Talford Starbuck—although in prison anything was possible. Still, this possibility had to exist only in Starbuck's mind. They wanted to tease him, and the poor man, in his innocence, had misunderstood completely and had escaped into Phillip's room in the hope of being given sanctuary. Well, why not? Starbuck had threaded his bobbin; Phillip could, at the least, rescue him from being raped—or, more likely, from the fear of being raped.

He waved toward the window. In response, Folger moved his head so that Butte could get a better view. They both continued to stare, only now more patient than puzzled.

"Is it okay then if I do something?" Starbuck asked.

"Like what?"

"This." Starbuck took a step toward Phillip, reached his arms around him, pulled himself close to his chest, rested his right cheek on Phillip's shoulder, and squeezed him.

Phillip's arms lifted from his sides in reflex, one hand holding the violin, the other the bow and the Milky Way. He was not so much surprised as stunned. Talford Starbuck was taking liberties for which others far more qualified would have given, if not years, at least several months, of their lives. In hopes of being permitted to embrace Phillip Manrahan, there had been in earlier years, expensive dinners, Rolex watches, concert tickets, and a laptop; there had been offers of financial settlements, divorce from a dutiful wife, and once the lure of a trip to Key West.

Because of his height, Phillip still had an unobstructed view of the door. Butte, at the moment of the embrace, had given his head a jerk backward, then moved it even closer to the glass. Folger turned away a bit so he could see out the side of his eye.

"No," Phillip said evenly, "I don't think you can do this."

Starbuck relaxed the squeeze but continued his hold. "Could you put your arms across my back, like you were holding me?"

"I am holding a violin and a candy bar and a violin bow, and I think it's about as much as I can do."

37

"Just for a second. Your arms, not your hands. Across my back. Then I'll let go. I promise."

Phillip glanced toward the window. Butte was slack-jawed with disbelief, Folger more skeptical, his eye narrowed and still looking sideways. Each was, in his own way, entranced, hardly a negligible achievement. Phillip could not resist amazing them further. He moved the violin from side to side to make sure he had their attention. Then he swallowed, took a breath, looked directly at Butte, at Folger, and reached his arms across Starbuck's back, the candy bar, the violin, and the bow dangling from the young man's shoulder blades.

Starbuck's hair smelled like Old Spice shaving lotion, and Phillip suspected he put it on to save the trouble of giving himself a shampoo. The young man's nose was poked deeper into Phillip's chest, and he had the feeling there'd be a small streak of snot left behind to mark the spot.

Butte and Folger had both pulled a few inches away from the window, the better to observe the embrace, but when they moved their heads back, they knocked temples, separated, then came together more carefully, completely absorbed in the sight of Phillip Manrahan's handsome arms across Talford Starbuck's unworthy back.

"Okay," Starbuck whispered. "I'm going to let go now. You can let go too. Okay?"

The two men let go of each other, and when Starbuck didn't step back, Phillip did, letting the violin, the candy bar, and the bow rest against his sides. He glanced down at his shirt. Sure enough, there were two moist and sticky spots commemorating the meeting between his chest bone and Starbuck's nose.

"Thanks," the young man whispered. "I'll go in a couple of seconds. They won't bother me now."

"You sure they were bothering you?" Phillip put the violin and bow on his bunk next to Aggie's letter and the candy bar on the shelf next to the toilet.

"I should have known better," Starbuck said. "These pants."

Phillip looked at Starbuck's pants. In shop, Starbuck had "tailored" them. If he had wanted to make a particular display of his buttocks, he had succeeded. They looked like two well-inflated footballs, one pressed next to the other between the slender hips.

Phillip was beginning to understand. To Butte and Folger this could seem an enticement, and they were now expecting Starbuck to make good on the invitation he had offered. Prison protocol—codified by the inmates and as minutely detailed as any charter set down by Napoleon or Hammurabi, and even more immutable—specified that there were jocks and there were marks, and that marks submitted to jocks. Butte and Folger, with their unceasing athleticism, had identified themselves as jocks. And the unthinking Starbuck had, with his tailored pants, declared himself a mark. Butte and Folger were simply about to exercise their rights, and it could not be expected that Starbuck could refuse. He had, with the willful restitching of his pants, placed himself in a well-defined social category. If he denied his status and resisted the attendant activity, he could be found guilty of "playing hard to get" and sentenced accordingly. The punishment would then be carried out by every inmate devoted to justice and interested in Talford Starbuck's ass.

Phillip, however, was left with a question, and he decided to ask it. "Starbuck, just how do I figure in this?"

"I had to prove I wasn't lying." Starbuck looked down at the floor, wiggled his toes inside his shoes, then looked up at Phillip. "I told him you were my jock and they should leave me be." His eyes moved sideways; his head tilted a little to the left. "And is it okay? Can you try not to look like you're mad at me?"

The Milky Way now made sense. A mark always brought gifts to his jock. If the jock was on drugs, the offerings were, quite simply, drugs. If the jock was not on drugs it was usually with a Pepsi, a bag of potato chips, a candy bar, a pack of cigarettes, that the conjugal gesture was most often made. Apparently Phillip was to pose as Starbuck's protector, their troth pledged by a Milky Way.

Starbuck was moving to Phillip's left, then went past him so that

Phillip had to turn around to see what he was up to. "Now where are you going?"

"They can see my face instead of yours." He smiled up at Phillip, a smile he must have assumed was seductive, but which came across as the grin of a near idiot.

"Starbuck, you're a nice kid, but you don't need me to help you. They're not going to do anything to you."

With the leer still on his face, Starbuck said, "But they could kill me."

"What do you mean, kill you? They're probably not even going to hurt you."

"But I could die from what they're going to do. I've seen it happen. Evan, my friend Evan, my best friend, he died from it. I was there. I saw it happen when he died. You die from it." He grabbed Phillip's other arm and gave it a shake, the young man's strength so unsuspected that Phillip didn't pull away. "They're still there," Starbuck continued. "They're still watching. They still don't believe about you and me. Kiss me. That'll do it. Kiss me."

"No, I don't think I'm going to do that."

"Please? I promise I'll keep my mouth closed."

Starbuck reached up, flung his arms around Phillip's neck, and pulled his head down. Even as Phillip tried to tug free, Starbuck crushed his lips just to the side of Phillip's mouth. Without taking the lips away, he muttered, "Don't move yet. Please. Count three, both of us. One—"

Phillip made no move. That Talford Starbuck had had the gall, the guts, or whatever to grab at his privileged neck and force his enviable head down to his own level had Phillip completely immobilized. And the idea that Talford Starbuck had his lips pressed near Phillip's treasured mouth made Phillip want to reject not Starbuck's flesh but his own, to be rid of it since it had been so fouled by this importuning. And there, at his door, peering in as at a peep show, were Roger Butte and Jason Folger, and here was he, Phillip Manrahan, caught in the desperate embrace of Talford Starbuck, the resident absurdity. He, Phillip Manrahan, the aloof and dignified mystery of Tier Two, pulled into this repellent performance—and for the benefit of the prison's two masters of mockery.

Phillip could either fling Starbuck away and vomit all over him—which he was quite capable of doing—or he could frustrate Butte and Folger by pretending that he was not overwhelmed with disgust, that Starbuck was acting well within his rights to yank at Phillip's neck and slobber against his mouth.

To rob Butte and Folger of their satisfaction, to bewilder their eager faces, seemed a greater reward than the punishment of Starbuck. And so Phillip reached up his arms and pulled Talford Starbuck even closer. He raised a hand and placed it on the back of the young man's head. He moved his lips to Starbuck's right cheek. He could smell the earwax, a blunt, dull scent that seemed to have its origins in turnips and cabbage.

"Good," Starbuck muttered. "Three." Having completed the count, he started to pull away, but Phillip held on. He tightened his grip, especially on the back of Starbuck's head, and dug his fist into his spine. "It's okay now," Starbuck whispered. "They've seen enough."

It was only when Phillip's nose caught again the scent of Old Spice, smelling now like apple pie, that he loosened his hold and moved a little away from Starbuck. "Are your friends still there?" he asked.

Before Starbuck could answer, there was a knock on the door. Phillip looked over his shoulder. Butte's knuckles were rapping on the window. He wiggled his fingers, more like scratching at the glass then a wave, then knocked again. Folger's head shoved Butte's aside, and he too rapped, waved, then rapped again. He was beaming. Obviously he had enjoyed the show and wanted now to shake Phillip's hand and congratulate him. Then Butte's face took over the window, but it was immediately obscured by the waving hand, more enthusiastic than before. Now both his fingernails and Folger's fingernails were tapping on the glass, a prison equivalent, perhaps, of an ovation.

Phillip considered doing an encore as if he and Starbuck had been asked to reprise their impassioned scene. But then, it might be even more interesting to invite them in, to let them solemnly state their acceptance of Phillip as Starbuck's jock—Phillip and Starbuck hooked up, which meant, according to the infrangible inmates' code, that no one else would touch him, the sanctity of mutual commitment more rigidly respected within prison confines than without.

But they would, of course, bring with them into the room their own brand of contempt. They would be hearty and friendly. They would do their best to convince both Phillip and Starbuck that they considered it an honor to have been witnesses to their conjugal exercise. But they would make it clear, at the same time, that the very idea of Phillip and Starbuck hooked up was disgusting beyond measure. Still, that, too, could be interesting.

Phillip started toward the door.

"Don't! Please!" Starbuck swung around and stood in front of Phillip. "Let me talk first. They'll make you say you didn't mean it."

"But I didn't mean it."

Starbuck sucked in a breath, then spoke in a high-pitched voice as he exhaled. "They'll make you laugh at what we did."

Phillip tilted his head to one side. "I won't laugh. Believe me."

"They'll say we were only making believe. They'll take me away. I'll get skinny and go blind and crazy and I'll keep shitting all the time. I've seen it. I'll be all alone and covered with shit and I'll die. Please. Don't let 'em in. You're the one can save me."

"That's ridiculous. Hook up with somebody else."

"Who? Nobody else is old like you. There's nobody like you I'd be safe with. Nobody who will just hang around with me and make everyone else think we're really hooked up. You're the only one on the tier old like this. You've got to help me."

Phillip drew his shoulders back, slowly. Starbuck had hardly resorted to the proper method of persuasion. Phillip, if he weren't so repulsed by the young man in front of him, would have shown him exactly how old he was. The method would not have been gentle.

And yet, he could not help hearing what Starbuck had said. Phillip was in his early fifties, a truth he never avoided for the simple reason that he never gave it any thought. For him, birthdays were celebrated, not accumulated. He was unburdened by the years because he simply shed them as they passed. He considered himself lean; his face had surely taken on "character" rather than age, and the lines that framed his mouth with parentheses made his lips—he was certain—even more promising than before.

Although he had withdrawn from the sexual scene, he had never considered it forced retirement. Not until now, at the sound of Talford's remark, had he considered that age itself—his age—was at issue when sexual choices were being made. In all honesty, he had blithely assumed that he could come out of retirement at any time, much to the relief of those who had been denied his attentions during the dry season his withdrawal had imposed. For him, this had not been an article of faith; it was an axiomatic fact. It was so far removed from question that doubt was unimaginable. He was the same tall, lean, blond, brown-eyed paragon he had become during his teenage years. Gifted to the point of genius, mathematician, athlete, musician, amiable by effort and considerate by choice, he bestowed pleasure wherever he went. Any event was elevated by his presence, by his participation. At times, of course, he could be somewhat shy, but that was only to protect himself from all the ready attentions that might overwhelm him, all the importunings that were about to descend upon his favored head. Shyness, he knew, assumed that there was an inordinate interest on the part of others—when it wasn't his own cover-up for rapacious demands and salacious intents. Fortunately, those ignorant of its true origins mistook shyness for humility, when it was quite the opposite—and found in it an added charm. Even his defects had improved upon his seeming perfections.

But perhaps the days of his excellence had come and gone. Perhaps the time had come—as it must—when he must rely on the clouded vision of the beholder. But surely this could not be. Not yet. Phillip looked directly at the young man who, in turn, was searching Phillip's face. He seemed to have a particular interest in Phillip's forehead. But after seeming to give wary attention to Phillip's hairline and the cresting hair above it, he looked down again at his feet, and wiped his nose on his sleeve.

"I don't want to shit all over myself," he whispered. "Please. I really don't." He shook his head and continued to look at his shoes.

Butte and Folger were still at the door. Phillip would have liked to smash the glass right into their overeager faces. Instead, he, too, looked down at Starbuck's shoes. "All right," he said quietly. "As far as anyone else is concerned, we're hooked up."

Starbuck started to raise his head, but nodded instead. "And don't worry," he said. "Lots of you straight guys hook up. It doesn't mean you're still not straight."

"Who's straight?"

Starbuck looked up. He stared into Phillip's face, slowly adjusting to something he hadn't seen before—and wasn't quite sure he was able to see now. "Oh," he said. "Sorry. No offense. I thought you were straight."

Phillip decided to shrug. "But all we do is pretend, right?"

Again Starbuck had to stare into Phillip's face, this time completely uncomprehending. After he'd blinked twice, he said, "Of course all we do is pretend. What else would we do?"

Phillip felt a tightening in his muscles but told himself to just relax.

THREE

Rachel's illness began the day Mrs. Levo, a parishioner, beat her. Mrs. Levo's son, Tony, had been one of the children killed in the school fire. Rachel's upper lip had been cut, her left eye blackened, and the skin broken on her right cheek. There were bruises on her back and upper arms. Her chin, nose, and forehead were skinned from hitting the carpet, and her right wrist was sprained by the fall. It was on that night, the night after the beating, that Rachel had been found wandering through the gutted school, her garb torn away, her body—her face, her arms, her hands—smeared with soot from the charred ruins. Although Rachel herself—because of her cure—could remember very little of the beating and nothing of the night wanderings, she had some other memory, dim, remote, glimpsed more than experienced, and it was this particular moment that she had chosen to mark the beginning of her affliction.

She was in the parlor of the parish rectory, waiting for the pastor, Father Costello. As Sister Superior of the school, she had come with a proposal that Anna Ballestrero, a graduating eighth-grader, give the graduation speech instead of Father Boyd. Anna was highest in the class, and Rachel thought Father Boyd, the catechist for the sixth, seventh, and eighth grades, had already said as much as he might have to say. It would be a break with tradition, but Rachel felt rather strongly that her students should be made aware that the time had come for them to begin articulating their own thoughts and feelings. If the received education was to be praised, it would be more seemly if the praise came from one of the educated rather than from one of the educators.

Father Costello would oppose the suggestion; Rachel would calmly expand upon her reasonings; Father Costello would dismiss the suggestion; Rachel would make a case for experiment; Father Costello would become thoughtful in a disgruntled way; Rachel would praise his flexibility, his ability to explore the new and the untried; Father Costello would continue being thoughtful, but would become less disgruntled; Rachel would then show herself near-awed by his courage, by his singular belief in the children of his school; Father Costello would become befuddled; Rachel would be moved and grateful that she was allowed to serve under a man of his wisdom and daring—and would quickly leave the room before the priest could reflect on his presumed acquiescence.

Waiting for Father Costello that afternoon in the rectory parlor, Rachel was looking at the picture on the far wall, above the couch. It was *The Last Supper*, but not by Leonardo. The general grouping was pretty much the same, everyone conveniently huddled on one side of the table, with Jesus in the middle, blessing the bread, a dark brown loaf that looked like pumpernickel. Everyone in the painting was looking at the bread except Judas and a cat. Judas was shielding his face, his cloak drawn up to his right ear, possibly to fend off the sacred words of consecration. The cat, gray and whiskered, sitting on its haunches, was looking straight ahead, out of the painting, directly at Rachel. Often Rachel on other visits to the rectory had wondered what the cat was doing there, looking at her like that. Was it a joke? Was it homage to a wealthy patron's prized cat? A theological assertion that cats and all their kind were not active participants in the redemptive Eucharist taking place behind it? A humanizing domestic inclusion?

On this particular day, the cat seemed even more present than usual, and Rachel felt obliged to understand at last why it was there and what it was doing. Was the cat scornful? No. Was it interested in Rachel? Definitely not. Then why was it looking at her? Rachel stared back, trying to seem equally uninterested. Meeting on this common ground, perhaps she and the cat might come to an understanding of what was going on between the two of them. Rachel looked at the cat, and the cat looked at Rachel. Neither moved, neither blinked. Until, of course, Rachel herself blinked, and moved her hand from her lap and stretched it out toward the painting. But she had not lost the contest; she had won. She understood at last.

The cat, sitting there, staring, was trying to prevent Rachel from looking beyond it, suggesting that she see only itself, the cat, and be distracted, even satisfied, and feel no need to see the surrender of body and of blood taking place beyond it, in the painting. The cat was there to take to itself all surmise and speculation, allowing Rachel to concentrate on its presence and its pose rather than be aghast at the abject corporeal love being offered a few feet away.

The cat was there to spare Rachel the sight of the young man's invitation to make his body, his blood, a part of her own body, her own blood. The cat was there to come between Rachel and the realization that the divine was to be experienced through the flesh, that God at this moment was making known his wish, his command, that he participate in nature's given course as an eaten chunk of common bread.

Surely this was sacrilege; this was blasphemy. But it was true. God, creator, redeemer, had agreed, for his love's sake, to mingle, ultimately, through bread and through wine, with human waste. He was willing to become—the words from Gedney Street where she'd grown up came rushing back before she had time to stop them—willing to become shit and piss. This man in the painting, blessing the bread, was the first blasphemer, and the last. He was the first to commit sacrilege, and after him sacrilege was impossible. Nothing could be done to his flesh and his blood that could surpass his own willing degradation. He had come to participate in the piss and shit of the world, and who, after him, after this, could humiliate or defile him? All efforts would be petty and pathetic. Nothing could be done to him that he himself had not already agreed to, and willingly.

Do not look at this blasphemer, do not witness this sacrilege: that was what the cat was saying. The cat was there as Rachel's protector. She must look at the cat and not at the young man and the pumpernickel bread. The cat would rescue her from her own disgust, from her own appalling thoughts. And from the thrill of returned love she felt at the sight of this complete submission. In mercy, the cat would come between her and this man's act of absolute love. She would not see it. She would not know it. She would be spared.

Rachel had gotten up from her chair and was moving toward the painting, her hand reaching out. But what the hand was intending to touch, she did not know. Her veil brushed against a statue on the table next to the couch and knocked it over. It was the thunk of the hollow plaster onto the carpet that made her stop. And, in stopping, she was able to hear the siren and the blared honking of a fire engine going past outside. A fire engine was a cause for curiosity, but not much more. But when the siren stopped within her hearing, she felt the first nudge of terror, a quick ripple along the surface of her skin. She looked toward the window. The back end of a fire truck was visible. Two firemen were jumping down, still buckling their rubber coats.

She lurched toward the parlor door and caught her skirt on the arm of a chair. She ripped it free. Her elbow knocked against a lamp, then against the doorjamb as she went through. Father Costello was coming down the hall toward the parlor. "Fire," Rachel whispered. "Fire."

What happened after that—the fire itself, the sixth-graders trapped with young Sister Louise in the basement lunchroom, Rachel's later visits to the parents of the dead, the beating by Mrs. Levo—all this Rachel could sometimes remember, but because of her cure, it was like something that had been written about her, that she'd read, but hadn't experienced. It might bring horror, but in a protected way. Her sympathies were real, but they were general. There would be smoke, but not the smell of smoke; fire, but no heat. The cries could be heard, but they failed to stab her eardrum and pierce through into her brain.

Her cure, effected by electroconvulsive shock therapy, had managed to round up all these memories as if they were a marauding rabble, then consign them to an enclosed territory where they could no longer endanger her memory or overthrow her mind. They existed, and Rachel could make herself aware of them when she wanted to, but—also because of her cure—she seldom wanted to. They were a part of her history, but no longer a part of her life.

What had been obliterated completely, however, was Rachel's memory of the night she went back into the burned-out school, the night after she'd been assaulted by Mrs. Levo. She had been made to forget as well the afternoon three days later when, in the hospital, her brother Phillip had come to see her. The whole idea of the visit had, at the time, distressed her. She wasn't sick; she needed some rest, and now that she'd had it—for three days—she was ready to leave. She'd also objected when told that, instead of going back to St. Michael's, to her school and her convent, she would spend some time at the Motherhouse. In that instance, she had been bound by her vow of obedience, but, regarding her brother's visit, she felt she should be free to make her own decision. Still, Dr. Zaug—precise, thoughtful Dr. Zaug—had encouraged her to see Phillip. And Rachel had finally agreed, but only after Dr. Zaug, sitting there in her room, carefully pushing back the cuticles of his fingernails, had explained that Phillip had to be consulted about her treatment, and his permission given for the therapy they'd prescribed. Phillip, after all, had received permission from her Order not only to pay for her treatment, but to involve himself in the decisions that had to be made. And since he would be there consulting with Dr. Zaug, some time with his sister should certainly be allowed.

After Dr. Zaug had left, Rachel did nothing for a moment: she simply sat there. Then she drew her hand up and touched the bruise below her eye. She looked at the hospital gown she was wearing, then at her arms, bare from the elbow down. She looked at her unshaven legs, the hair darker than the hair on her arms. Rachel drew her feet back under her chair, then crossed her arms, trying with her hands to cover as much of herself as she could.

After another moment, she slowly unfolded her arms and let her feet come forward. She must not be vain. She must not be too proud to let her brother see her as she was. Quiet tears came to her eyes. She let them run down her cheeks until they began dripping onto the front of her hospital gown, dampening her chest.

It hurt when she blotted the dresser scarf onto her cheeks. But she let herself cry some more, then smoothed the scarf back across the top of the dresser, pushing down hard with the palm of her hand where the cloth was bunched and crinkled. She sat down to see if the tears would come again. When they didn't, she touched the bone beneath her eye. It still hurt.

She stared carefully into the mirror. She saw the face of Mrs. Buchanan, who had come to the convent one night to escape from her husband who had beaten her because, at supper, the potato he'd put in his mouth—whole—was too hot. Just like Mrs. Buchanan's, Rachel's eyes, receding back into the skull, were circled with black, the black leaking into purple, yellow, and green farther down the cheek. There was a lump on the upper lip, where she'd been cut by Mrs. Levo's wedding ring, and a scab was forming on her jaw. Across her forehead was a deep scratch, and some of the flesh on her left cheek was still shredded where Mrs. Levo had clawed with her fingernails.

On top of her head there was a burst of cropped black hair, sticking almost straight up, except at the sides, where it sprang out over her ears. She combed her fingers through the hair, but it did no good.

Never could she let her brother see her this way.

When, stammering, whispering, she asked Stella, the hospital attendant, if she had something that might cover the bruises and cuts, the woman misunderstood and thought she was asking for bandages. To explain, Rachel cleared her throat and said the word "makeup" as clearly as she could. Stella promptly brought some pancake, which Rachel thought smelled like roses mixed with lard. Gently Stella did her best, spreading on a fairly thick layer that made Rachel's face feel greasy and flushed, as if she'd been cooking something in a steaming pot.

When Rachel whispered, "lipstick," Stella fetched her own and again applied enough to cover the cut. She told Rachel she looked beautiful now. Rachel smiled a quick smile, opening the cut on the lip again. She touched it with her wrist to stop the blood. When she stared at the imprint the lipstick had made, she saw, wet within it, a small dot of blood, its red no match for the crimson around it. She continued to stare until Stella raised her face to touch up her lips and cover again the opened wound.

Stella, her fingers lightly holding up Rachel's chin, examined her handiwork. She tilted her head, pursed her lips, then said, "Fine, Sister. Just fine. Can't see hardly a thing."

"Thank you," Rachel whispered.

After Stella had closed the door behind her, Rachel turned and looked at herself in the mirror. There in the glass was her likeness. Of that there could be no doubt. Except that this was not so much herself as a picture of her that might have been drawn and colored with crayons by a fourth-grader. The outline of her head had been nicely sketched, but the same crayon—orange—had been used to color her entire face. There was some shading where the bruises leaked through, but even they were made to seem no more than a deeper orange. And onto this surface her eyes, nose, and mouth had been drawn, forgetting her eyebrows and eyelashes altogether. The eyes were small and dark, peering out from inside the skull, as through the openings in a Halloween mask. Her mouth was huge. Stella had thoughtfully accommodated the cut on the upper lip, then enlarged the entire mouth to make it proportionate and perfect.

Rachel looked at herself for more than a few minutes. The fourth-grader, she judged, was of medium talent, with an obvious interest in lips and a fondness for the color orange. But what she saw also was a passable likeness and she must not complain. And besides, perhaps the artist, as so often happens, had seen a truer self not readily perceived by others. This could be the more actual Rachel whether she approved or not. Still, she allowed herself to lower the blind and turn on only the lamp on the bed stand.

She put on the unstarched pale green dress the hospital had provided; the alternative would have been to wear the blue flowered gown, the one that tied in back and kept the patient prepared for bedpans, back rubs, and hypodermic needles. The green dress' only concession to style was a pocket on the left side. It had no collar and no belt. Rachel's neck felt bare, her waist undisciplined. She wondered what she might put into the pocket other than her hand.

To make herself feel less exposed, Rachel put her rosary around her neck, the crucifix resting just below her throat. She had nothing with which to cincture her waist, but into the pocket she decided to put her toothbrush, toothpaste, and an oatmeal cookie left from lunch. This, perhaps, might prove that she was living an active and varied life. To give some indication that she was still a nun—and to tame her obstreperous hair—she slipped the pillow case from her pillow, placed it in a band across her forehead, drew the edges behind her, and pinned them together at the nape of her neck. Not a true veil, but it would do.

She had been given leather-soled brown sandals and white ankle socks, leaving her legs still bare. She considered getting into bed so she could cover herself with the blanket, but she didn't want to seem sick. She'd just pull her feet back under the chair. That way, her legs—and the dark curling hair—might not be noticed after all. About her arms she could do nothing. She'd already decided against a bathrobe. The arms would have to stay bare. It occurred to her that what had been teenage vanities—her fine neck, her well-formed legs, her smooth unblemished skin, the delicate ears—were now mortifications, an embarrassment she must accept.

Waiting for Phillip, she looked around the room. There was the bed, high and narrow, with a white spread designed and sewn into the crinkled and scalloped pattern of a Venetian curtain so that it could never be smoothed, nor could it appear wrinkled. There was the bed stand with the lamp. The lamp shade, made of what looked like oiled parchment, had a picture of a man on a horse jumping over a high green hedge. The man was wearing a red coat and white pants, the pants stuffed into high black boots. There was a small dog, brown, longhaired, half-crouched, its bushy tail rising behind it as if the dog wanted to be a squirrel. The sky was tan. Perhaps blue would not have been masculine enough. Rachel made sure the picture side of the lamp shade was facing the chair where Phillip would sit. He'd have something to look at other than herself. To complete the decoration, Rachel stood her missal, prayer book, and a small black book of meditations in a row on the dresser. Books always made a room look more comfortable.

She sat down in her chair and folded her hands dutifully on her lap. She was staring at the knuckle of her right thumb when she heard a light but rapid tapping on the door, as if a meeting of chipmunks was being called to order. This would be her brother Phillip. Peppy. She tried to say "come in" but her throat had dried. She swallowed three times, and then the door opened, inward, a little more than halfway.

There, standing behind Stella, was a man who looked like Rachel's father. But he was even more handsome than she'd remembered, his unruly blond hair—corn colored, really—tumbling in plumed folds down onto his ears, with one lock curling toward his left eye as if he were a movie star. His hair was longer, his nose had become leaner, his mouth more full, and he had grown a moustache. He was looking at her, and from the way the ends of his mouth twitched, trying to lift themselves, she could tell he was trying to smile. He had obviously come to take her home, back to the house on Gedney Street where they'd all lived together—he and her mother and her brother George and the baby, Phillip—before her father had drowned, and her mother too, in the river when her mother got a cramp and her father had tried to rescue her. And now he had come to her from the land of the drowned, and all their lives would begin again.

Her father was staring at her with wide, unblinking eyes. Maybe he couldn't even see her. He was just standing there, staring. But when he finally spoke, his voice was a dry whisper, rasping along his throat.

"Aggie?" he said.

"No, not anymore," Rachel said. "I'm Sister Rachel now. Can't you tell?"

"It's Peppy."

"You're Peppy?"

"Phillip. Your brother."

Rachel stared long at the man standing there. Gradually the features reformed themselves, but only slightly. Yes, this would be Peppy. He was taller than their father, more perfectly built. It was as if the infusion of their mother's genes had effected some final refinement, the last evolutionary step from the strong and stocky peasant to the lean and muscular athlete. His eyes were dark, like his father's, but less troubled. They seemed, as she remembered, just a little out of alignment with each other, giving them a slightly disordered look, as if he were trying to avoid capture, one eye always on the lookout for an ambush that might overtake him at any moment. She must reassure him. She must comfort him. She must convince him that no harm would ever come to him, that she, Aggie, his sister, would never permit it.

"Peppy, yes, come in. Please. You must sit down, in here, with me. See? There's the chair, just for you. I told them to bring it. Come in. Sit down here, with me."

Phillip moved slowly past her, careful not to touch her chair or her skirt. He sat down, put his hands on his lap, then shifted his right arm and placed it on the bed, his hand open on the spread. "I brought you some lilacs," he said. "They'll bring them to you. When they find a vase. So they can put them in water."

Rachel nodded. When neither said anything for what seemed a full minute, Rachel asked, "Do I smell?"

Her brother scrunched up his face. "No. Of course not. That's not why I brought them. The lilacs. You don't smell at all. You like lilacs. They're your favorite."

"Oh. I thought maybe I smelled. I have this—on my face, on my mouth—I have this salve." For whatever reason she couldn't admit it was makeup. "It's salve. There was a fire."

"Yes. I came when they had the funerals. Remember?"

"You did? Did I see you there?"

"It isn't important."

Rachel turned away. She should have remembered. She looked first at the floor, then at the light switch on the wall, then at the cord of the drawn blinds on the window. "I remember there was a fire. In the school," she said. "That's why I worry I might smell. That's why I'm here, in the hospital, because there was a fire. That's why I had to come here." She stared briefly at her brother's hand on the bedspread, then at the caster on the leg of the bed. "I'm not burned. Not anything like that. I didn't get hurt. Not at all." She glanced at the molding along the baseboard, then at her ankle, at the white sock, the sandal, the toe of her sock poking through. "Not even the smoke hurt me. I tried—I wanted—I mean, no, I'm all right. I'm fine. I don't know why they sent me here. Look. My arms. Nothing. My legs even. That's why I wear these clothes. So everyone can see. Do you see anything burned?"

"No. But your face, near your eye—"

"It's the salve. That's all it is. Salve." One inch at a time, Rachel leaned back in the chair until her shoulder blades touched the wood. Her upper torso sprang forward, but she caught herself, then slowly leaned back again, this time allowing the wood to touch her. "See? I'm fine."

"Yes. I see." He was looking at her face. He lowered his head, then turned and looked toward the window. "I wonder when they'll bring the lilacs."

"They have to find a vase."

"Yes."

They were both looking at the drawn blind, Rachel at the lower slats, Phillip at the cord. Then Phillip glanced down at his hand on the bedspread. He rubbed the hand back and forth, like a blind man trying to erase a message he'd just read.

"It's wonderful here, though," Rachel said. "They're so good, the way they take care of you. I mean, me."

"Good. I'm glad."

"They let you sleep as long as you want. It doesn't even bother them. You can sleep half the morning, they don't care. And the food, you can eat it or not eat it. Maybe a little word about another try with the carrots, but they don't really care. You can stand or sit, kneel or lie down. They let you. You can keep quiet or, if you want to, you can scream. Yes. Scream. Here. I'll show you."

Twice she screamed, her mouth, distorted and pulled taut, her eyes slitted and terrified. Her whole body rose and fell; it expanded and contracted as if she were trying to empty herself of all breath, of all strength.

"Don't. Please, don't. You'll hurt yourself." Phillip reached over and touched the tips of his fingers lightly on the back of her hand.

"See? They let you if you want to. Would you like me to do it again?"

"No. No, it's all right."

"I scared you, didn't I? I didn't mean to. Why would I do that? You have to learn not to be scared. Not of anything. Even if I scream." She began to open her mouth, readying herself to do it again. Phillip held out his hand toward her. Slowly she closed her mouth and slowly Phillip lowered his hand and let it rest just above his knee. He had straight, thin creases in his pants legs; they were so neatly pressed. It was a suit he was wearing, and a tie too. His hand was big and strong.

"They—Dr. Zaug, actually—" Phillip said, "Dr. Zaug says they have a—a procedure is what they call it—that can make you better. A treatment. You're going to have it, a whole series, beginning tomorrow, if I give permission. It won't hurt. You won't feel it at all. And it'll help you get better. Is that all right with you?"

"I am better. I'm always better after I scream."

"But after they give you this—this treatment—you won't have to scream."

"Yes, I will. I'll always have to scream. Nothing can change that."

"It'll make it so you won't even want to scream."

"Oh no. Please. Please, don't let them take away my screams. I need them. I don't know what I'd do if I thought they wouldn't be there when I need them. Please, don't let them. Believe me, I have to have them!"

"But you scream because you're in pain. They'll take away the pain."

"I'm not in pain. Really, I'm not. It's just—just that I'm so—lost."

"Lost?"

"No, not me. The children. I couldn't find them. I knew they'd been there. I heard them, yelling, calling me. That's why I scream. To answer them. To let them know I'm looking for them, even if I can't find them."

"This will all be over—soon. I'll tell Dr. Zaug it's all right to—I'll give him my permission to—"

"No, don't tell the doctor anything. Don't let him do anything. I know what to do. I'll go there again and again. To the school. And you mustn't worry about me. I'm all right there. All the fires are out. Dead. Even the fires. Dead."

"Yes, I know, but—"

"No you don't know! Because you've never been there. Neither have I. They're the only ones who've been there." She looked up quickly, frightened, staring at him. "You haven't been there, have you? Tell me. You haven't—" She put her arm across her eyes as if to protect them, to keep them from seeing. "Black wood," she said. "Burned stones." Her voice was toneless, as if she were too emptied to give her words inflection. "Everything black. Everything cold. No one there. I put my hands, my face, against the stones, against the burned wood. I broke off chunks of smoke, to eat it. I ate as much as I could, shoving it into my mouth, but I couldn't swallow anymore. It spilled out, all over me. It got my clothes dirty, the smoke I couldn't eat. My clothes, they were all dirty."

Phillip lowered his head. His hair fell forward, over his eyes. He didn't move. "Don't, Aggie. Please."

Rachel moved her arm away from her eyes and looked at her brother. "Do you want to leave?" she asked. Phillip shook his head no without looking up. "I can be alone," Rachel said. "I was alone there. I can be alone here. I have to get used to it."

Phillip lifted his head, but didn't brush the hair from his forehead. His mouth began to open, but he closed it, shook his head again. "You're not alone, Aggie. I'm here."

Rachel seemed not to have heard. "So I took off my garb, my clothes," she continued. "They were all dirty with smoke. I loved my nun's habit. It was precious to me. It was my life. But I mustn't wear it, not anymore. I didn't deserve it. So I took it off. I tried not to cry, but my tears made my hands all wet, and the black soot, the smoke was smeared all over me. I took them—my clothes—all off. They were so beautiful. I laid them on a stone, near a black window that was broken. Gently, gently, I laid them down. I thought I might wipe my tears on the hem of my veil, but I knew I mustn't touch it, any of it, my good, my dear—my veil. My lovely, lovely veil—"

Rachel stopped and smoothed her hospital dress over her knees. "I left them there. It was so cold. I used the dried smoke to cover me. That would be my clothes. Smoke. Only smoke." She pressed her spread fingers across her forehead, forming a cage for her eyes. It was then that she heard the gagging sound. Her brother had thrown back his head, his eyes staring at the ceiling. His jaw was moving up and down, caught in a spasm. Then his scream came, but he stopped it before it could finish, before it could escape completely. Still gagging, he swallowed the scream, forcing it, gulp by gulp, back down, as if he wanted to swallow his throat.

Rachel took the spread fingers away from her forehead. "You can scream," she said. "We can both scream. Shall we? The two of us, together?"

"No. Please." His voice was low but firm. He started to say something more and to reach out his hand, but stopped when the hand was no more than a few inches from his knee. He raised his head and drew the skin of his face taut, back toward his ears. His mouth was rigid, his eyes slightly hooded as if he were looking down at her from a great height. He stood up, smoothed the arms of his suit, then hunched his shoulders and let them drop, just to make sure his suit was in place. "The treatment will help," he said. "The doctor promised."

Rachel, too, had stood up. "You're going? So soon?"

"I told Dr. Zaug I'd come to his office in half an hour. It's close to that now."

"But there might be things I want to tell you."

"What things?"

"I don't know. But there must be something."

"Next time."

Rachel waited a moment, then nodded her head. "Next time." After the second nod, she didn't raise her head. Phillip had opened the door and was standing there. She leaned her head toward him and looked desperately at his necktie, just below the knot, as if it were a microphone into which she must speak if she hoped to be heard. "When you pray," she said, "pray that there will be no fire. Ask God that the fire mustn't happen, that the—the children, that they'll be safe. That no harm will come to them, that they mustn't be frightened and they mustn't choke, they mustn't die. Please. Pray. Never the fire. Can you do that?"

"Aggie, it's too late. You mustn't talk like this. The fire is over. It happened, and nothing can change that. Not even God. You can't pray that it won't happen when it's happened already. So stop it. Just stop it."

"No! I won't stop it. We mustn't say only those prayers that can be answered. We must say those that can't. Those that are impossible. And we must pray them more fervently because they *are* impossible. Do it, Peppy. Forget that it can never be answered. Just do it. Please promise me!"

Now she would look up into her brother's eyes, away from the necktie and the knot. Which eye she would look into could be decided once she'd raised her head. But before she could make another move, Phillip, it seemed, was falling down right in front of her, collapsing in a heap there in the doorway. He was reaching out, obviously struggling to grab onto her. But then, quickly, before she could help him, he was up and out the door, and the door closed behind him. Rachel stood there. Then she realized what had happened. Her brother, in his pressed pants and handsome suit, had knelt down in front of her and had kissed the hem of her hospital gown. Her only thought was that this was a mental hospital, and behavior like that had to be expected.

FOUR

Phillip stepped up to home plate and knocked the tip of the bat against the sides of his shoes. He wasn't so much knocking whatever turf might be stuck to his cleats as he was acquainting his feet with the bat, reminding them that they were all in this together, that each was dependent on the other, and that he expected a unity of effort. They had their work cut out for them. Phillip was hardly anyone's first choice even for a no-account game between the second tier and the third tier. He was, as a matter of fact, the team joke. Although none of his teammates had said so out loud, his request that he be allowed to play was eagerly accepted by the twin captains, Folger and, of course, Butte, on the assumption that he would provide comic relief, that he could become the object of whatever jeers and laughter the spectators might have ready, and that a defeat could be blamed—good-naturedly—on Phillip's inclusion.

When he'd asked if he could join the game, Butte had put his hand on Folger's shoulder to silence whatever he'd started to say, and brought into use his most serious voice, which was always accompanied with a furrowed brow and a narrowed eye to indicate thought and sincerity. "You'd be willing to play on the team? You really would?"

This forced Phillip to repeat his offer. "Yeah. I'd like to play. If there's room."

"For you? Sure there's room. Plendy of room. Plendy." (The letter "t" was sometimes excised from Butte's alphabet and a "d" often made its replacement—as in "impordant," "muddafucka," and "plendy." His own name he pronounced "Bewd" as if it were the diminutive of "beaudiful.") Butte had put his arm around Phillip's waist and was walking him a few feet away from Folger. This would be his intimacy act, a scene scripted for the two of them alone, not even including Folger. If Phillip had been dealing with a bluebird or a robin, he would, in effect, have been taken under Butte's wing.

"That's terrific, you want to come onto the team. What position? First base, shortstop, outfield, you name it."

"Why don't you see how I am in practice?"

"Practice? Who practices? We don't practice, we *play*."

"I thought you practiced a couple of times a week."

"Naw. *That* wasn't practice. That was just to give Folger a chance to work off some of his fat." (Folger was lean to the point of emaciation.) Butte lowered his voice more in tone than in volume. This meant that what he was saying was for Phillip's ears alone. "Come next Tuesday. Good guys against bad guys. Us against them, our tier against turd. Start maybe outfield why don't you. Give you a chance to run around a liddle, get some exercise. Outfield, okay?"

Butte released his hold on Phillip. The exchange was over, Butte must now give his attention to other matters, like yelling to Dawson, a lesser member of the joyful band, telling him, "I'd bedder have some podado chips, right Dawson?" Which dispatched Dawson swiftly in the direction of the canteen.

Phillip had gotten the idea of playing baseball a month before. Since the afternoon he and Starbuck had hooked up, neither Butte nor Folger nor any other subscriber to the merry band had lost an opportunity to make a passing reference to sex or to age, usually when Phillip and Starbuck were together, but sometimes when either of them was alone.

The preferred theme of their mockery was Starbuck's presumed happiness. "Now *there's* a happy man. Just look at him. You ever see anyone happier than that? Someone sure knows how to make that man smile. Smile, sweetie. Show us how happy your Daddy makes you." Variations on the theme included Starbuck's presumed unhappiness. "He looks kind of down today. Maybe his Daddy couldn't do it so good last time. Sad, huh. I sure hope your Daddy's feeling better soon. But you got to expect days, man, when he needs his time off. He's got his strength to consider. Takes time sometimes. Just hang in there. For his sake, huh?"

Never was there any sarcasm in the tone in which these words were spoken. Every word was invested with a genuine concern. It was the absence of scorn that measured the depth of their mockery. There would be understanding hands on Starbuck's shoulder, touches on his cheek, even an arm around his waist, the taking of a hand, all the gestures of respectful caring. There were no sly smiles, no boisterous laughter, no winks, no nudges. They—Phillip and Starbuck—were to make no response to whatever was said. This, Phillip knew, would create a frustration among the merry men that would be the best revenge available. Comment about Phillip's prowess was not to be noted; references to Starbuck's happiness—or lack thereof—was not to be paid the least attention. Phillip had given Starbuck his instructions in this regard, and, while Starbuck was hardly the most apt pupil, he did manage at least to pretend to ignore what was being said.

At times, however, Starbuck took their remarks at face value, which, in its own way, could be troublesome. A week before, Starbuck, sitting on Phillip's bunk, had reported Folger's praise for his—Starbuck's—good looks, telling him he must really turn Phillip on, with a gorgeous face like his, lips you couldn't believe, a nose like nobody else's, and eyes—it must be the eyes that really got Phillip going. Starbuck had believed him. No one had ever spoken like that to him before. Nobody had ever seen the perfections in his face until now, and Starbuck was grateful almost to the point of awe. Phillip had neither the words nor the inclination to contradict what Folger had said, to explain to the young man that he'd been mocked, until Starbuck said with genuine perplexity, "How come you never say anything like that? You never tell me anything about how I look. How come?"

Instead of saying, "Because I cannot tell a lie," Phillip settled for, "I guess I don't have Folger's way with words, okay?" Starbuck, in mournful forgiveness, nodded his head, acknowledging and accepting Phillip's want of verbal skill.

It was, however, during a showing of the movie *Funny Face* in the television room that the idea came to Phillip that he wanted to play baseball again. He had played in college, the only accounting major on the team. It was a small school, granted, where baseball was all but buried beneath the hysteria for basketball, but he'd been a star player at outfield and had attracted enough notice to have a scout remark on his game, mentioning that a farm team might be interested if he was. He wasn't. He'd only played because his friend, Marty Aliota, was on the team and he'd wanted to be around Marty. Marty played first base, not a great hitter, but, being small, he could run faster than anyone else.

Marty was headed for Medical School at the State University and Phillip knew his own interest in the game would not survive Marty's departure from the field. He didn't like being on a team. He found camaraderie foolish and false; he thought the struts of the men in the locker room were as ridiculous as those of any deluded rooster; he considered the coach pathetic in his self-importance. He wanted to be with Marty, and since Marty had his own fascination for baseball, Phillip went along. To Marty, baseball, with all its pretensions to nuance and intellectual satisfaction, was still, at its core, the most savage of all American team sports. The brute force of football, he'd say, was the plunge of body against body, one intent on moving forward, the other on stopping the movement. It was about possession, ownership, territory, about doing anything that was allowed to keep and promote what one had, even if it was only an ovoid object of inflated pig's flesh and a few yards of torn turf. Basketball, Marty claimed, was also about possession and promotion, but the object was somewhat the opposite of football. Here the thrust of body on body was to be avoided, the skill involved the ability not to touch, but still bring the ball to its destined goal, its passage through a net whose bottom had been ripped away. Dr. Freud might have had his own thoughts about the need to crash a ball through a circle, to violate the hoop as often as possible, but Marty decided not to take up the subject; it was too obvious to be interesting.

In baseball, the touch was almost genteel. No more than a tag was needed, the lightest tap, and the defeat was absolute. Less brutal than football, less frenzied than basketball, baseball could promote itself as a sport more artful than the others. Yes, there were desperate runs and impossible catches; there were even injuries and squabbles, but that had to be expected. It was a game, and no game lacking the potential for injury was worth anyone's time of day. But, to many, baseball was leisurely, almost polite by comparison to its confreres. For Marty, however, baseball was about breaking skulls. It was a form of decapitation. The fury of the swung bat (*pace* Dr. Freud), the quick crack at the insolent ball—to Marty it was a head-bashing, a skull-cracking, the hit ball now a severed head. Every player played for that one moment, when the entire body was shot out into the protruding bat, then slammed full force against the defiant ball. The hit, the connection, the resounding crack were reward enough for whatever else had to be endured. The run from base to base and home again was merely a congratulatory progress, the triumphant journey celebrating the fraction of a second's achievement, the beaten skull, the high-flung head. It was a savagery deliciously disguised, conveniently removed from its actual origins.

Phillip lusted to play baseball again. But he pronounced himself idiotic the moment the idea came to him. For all his disdain, he had an extremely healthy respect for the dangers of the game, what it could do to even the most supple and fine-tuned body: the fierce runs and quick stops, the deadly projectile of the ball itself, the threats to muscle and tendon, the goad to reflex, the challenge to judgment. But the impulse came, and he had no inclination to ignore it.

Phillip and Starbuck had been in the television room, sitting against the back wall. Fred Astaire had just finished dancing with Audrey Hepburn. They were in Paris. He was a photographer, she a model. The purpose of the movie was to make Fred Astaire and Audrey Hepburn fall in love with each other, and, at the moment, the picture was doing fairly well at its task, given the color photography and the Parisian settings. (In this movie, out of respect for the near-androgynous character of its two stars, charm was substituted for sex.)

There weren't more than five or six inmates in the room. A few times a week Phillip put in an obligatory appearance there with Starbuck. While no hand-holding was expected, it was considered necessary for the two of them to sit side by side, proving that this was indeed a conjugal experience. Starbuck was more eager than Phillip for this mutual participation, but Philip, worried that any reticence on his part might be interpreted as a lack of energy, would throw himself into the incessant give-and-take that might convince all round them that they, Phillip and Starbuck, were a committed couple, Phillip, a low-rider in the company of his broad.

As Fred and Audrey were dancing, Bowersox was heard to say, "What's she doing with that old fart for? What does she want with him?" He was sitting up near the set. "He's too old for her. Look at him. All stick and no prick."

That he'd said this meant nothing to Phillip until Folger said, "Cool it. Daddy's here with Starry. You don't say things like that right in front of them. You know better, for shit's sake."

To that, Butte felt obliged to add, "Yeah, keep .it to yourself, why don't you?" Folger turned and looked at Phillip. "Don't pay any attention, okay? He didn't mean it. You guys go right ahead." The other men in the room promptly turned and looked at Phillip and Starbuck. No one said anything, but they all continued to stare until Starbuck, with quiet defiance said, "We're just looking at the movie is all."

Folger was the first to turn back in his chair. Fred Astaire was smiling at Audrey Hepburn, who wasn't sure if she would smile back or not. "Come on, guys," said Folger. "Watch the movie. It's for them to worry about, not us. Right?" The others now turned back toward the set. Starbuck slouched down in his chair, then drew himself up, raised his head an extra inch and watched the movie with even greater concern than before. Audrey Hepburn smiled at Fred Astaire.

It was then and there that Phillip decided he'd play baseball again. It was a stupid notion and he knew it. He hadn't played for over twenty-five years. How dumb could he be? He was in fair shape, no fat, no aches and pains, and his jogs around the track hadn't made him all that winded or set his heart pattering against his breastbone. But a man in his fifties does not usually take up baseball as his sport of choice. After all, that was why God had created golf. Still, Phillip was determined. He needed to play, not to prove his strength or his prowess—he might have none—but to take a swing again at the ball, to wham the bat forward with all his might, and connect. He wanted them—Butte and Folger and Dawson and Bowersox and the rest—to see him do it, swing, connect, crack, gone. He needed to do it and he would. Because he had to. Swing. Hit. Crack. Kill.

And so he began his preparations. Slowly, carefully, patiently, respectfully. After lockup and night count, in his room, lit only by the corridor light coming through the observation window in his door, naked, he began.

The wall was cold, the plaster coarse as he pushed, his body slanted into it, his heels lifting one at a time from the floor, bending one knee, then the other. He felt at first as if his purpose was to grind the plaster into the palms of his hands, but then the pain grew in his calves and he could tell that his Achilles' tendons were badly in need of stretching. Because this was his first session, he imposed patience and calm. His purpose was not to cripple himself, to tear and shred his muscles and bruise his bones. It was to stretch and limber the flesh, to give full life to a body already stiffening toward the rigor mortis that was to become its final experience. But not yet.

He grabbed hold of the toe of his right foot and pulled the leg up behind him until his heel hit against his buttock. Not too difficult to do, but the muscles in his front thigh protested anyway. They were being roused from a long and peaceful slumber, stretched awake and given notice that it would be a while before they'd sleep again. The protest continued as Phillip patiently awakened his left thigh as well.

One by one the old exercises were put back into use. The hamstrings in the backs of his thighs were reminded, in pain, of their existence. The muscles behind each knee, the back and shoulder muscles, were given the college treatment, the head was rolled as he tried to touch each shoulder with an ear. He lay prone, he lay supine, he sat, he squatted, he bent backward and forward, pulling, pushing, touching, still gentle, still patient, a slow-motion dance that summoned the body back to itself.

The first night was a fairly brief performance, a prologue to what was about to unfold on the nights to come. Later, with pain retained from the previous sessions, Phillip would begin again—and then again—night after night, the slow choreography that would reacquaint him with his flesh, remind him of the sinews and the bones, and summon again the obedient muscle and the welcome blood.

Only once did he overdo. In the second week, just as the pain was beginning to ease, Dawson had, that afternoon in the yard, asked Starbuck to wiggle his ears. When Starbuck said he didn't know how, Dawson reassured him that surely he could, with ears like that. Starbuck insisted he couldn't, and Dawson reached out and took hold of each ear and shook it. "See how easy it is? I can do it. I can wiggle your ears. Now you do it."

"I can't."

"Sure you can. See? Like this." Again he took hold and shook the ears, this time harder. Starbuck crinkled his nose and squinted his eyes. Phillip was about ten feet away, on the jogging track tying a shoe. "You could win contests," Dawson was saying. "Ears like yours, that's talent, man. Come on. Wiggle." He shook the ears even more furiously and Starbuck's helpless head with them. "That's it. Wiggle them ears, baby."

Phillip walked over, trying to saunter, but not quite managing it. "I don't think you're supposed to be touching him," he said.

Dawson stopped, released the ears, but let his hands hover near the sides of Starbuck's head. "Oh, hi Daddy. I guess I shouldn't've let you see me do that, huh?" He quickly took his hands away and put them on his chest in a gesture of guilty repentance. "Sorry. It was wrong and it won't happen again. But you can't blame me, can you? You know how tough it is not to touch. Us other guys, we get carried away, I guess. *You* can understand that. But I'll try not to let it happen again. When I start feeling I've got to touch, I'll just walk away. I'll keep my hands to myself." He reached out to touch the ear again, but stopped. "Ooops. There I go again. Just plain can't goddamn help it." Then, after a long inhale he turned and walked toward the handball court, shaking his head to dramatize how helpless he was in the face of such temptations.

Phillip bent down and retied his shoe. When he stood up, he was about to ask Starbuck if Dawson had hurt him, but Starbuck, leaning against the wall, was gazing in Dawson's direction. "I wish I *could* wiggle my ears," he said softly. "I tried, but I couldn't. He was disappointed, wasn't he?"

That night Phillip went into his exercises with a fury that made him punish rather than coax his body. He pushed too far too fast, and the body answered with an anger of its own. It tightened back into itself the next day. It rebelled by refusing to perform even ordinary tasks. It went on strike; it would not cooperate. A stride could become a limp, a bend was forbidden beyond a certain point, and attempted head movements, especially looking up, were refused outright. He had to give himself a few nights off.

It was on the second night of his enforced recess that he became aware of how much he missed the sessions, how bereft he felt. It was like the absence of a lover, the bedtime rites unobserved, the supple movements, the slow contortions, the extreme demands, the easy responses, the slow giving, all denied to him now. He had been wooing his body, but now his brute actions had caused refusal. He must begin again.

Which he did. Easy, slow, gentle, he took up his courtship again with a new respect, a more intense but more restrained fervor. And, after a few nights his body came back to him, tentatively at first, then with a growing response. The slow dance was resumed, the bent legs, the long reaches, the held pulls, the straining, the easing, now released, now taut, but always aware, even pleading gently for more.

Later, naked, sweating, lying on his bunk, he could feel the muted throb, the calling of the flesh, the plea not to be left alone in this awakened state. It was a suppliant's murmur. Phillip had teased his body back to life, awakened the slumbering flesh, and found that he loved it with an old and fervent yearning. What had, in his youth, been the vigorous, unthinking acceptance of its splendors, now became a deepened ardor, an ardor made sorrowful by its loneliness.

Like a boy he lay, all desire, but with no object for his yearning. His longing reached out into the great world, searching for that other to whom he might give this new found splendor, his body. His reach seemed infinite. But there was no one, there was only the journey and the reach and the unyielding world.

"Ball two!" The umpire, an inmate from the fourth tier named Scrimshaw, made the call as if he were surprised and a little disappointed at the pitcher's inability to put the ball within the confines that would define a strike. Phillip himself would have called it a strike, and was annoyed at Scrimshaw's partiality on his behalf. He was setting Phillip up for a walk in deference to his age.

It was the second inning but Phillip's first time at bat. In left field he'd made one out on a high fly ball that seemed to have been sent directly his way, and had also made a good throw to third for a second out. Exaggerated cries of praise from Folger, Butte, Dawson, Bowersox, and the other teammates—usually formed around the words "Daddydo" and "Daddydid"—had not amused him anymore than he had been amused by their "Show us how you do it, Daddy. Show us how you do!" When he'd first stepped up to the plate for his first strike, he whipped himself around, furious, and went down on his right knee. Butte, ever the self-appointed wit, was completely unable not to say, "On his knees, that's how he does it! Daddy on his knees is how he does it."

There was a scattering of applause among the twenty or so spectators hunched and squatted along the first base line. With their straggled hair, their oversized sweats and stretched T-shirts, with their baggy chinos and jeans, their stubble beards and untended moustaches, they looked like an ill-organized bunch of protestors come not to observe the game but to harass the players. An error provoked more enthusiasm than a hit or a run or good catch. Still, they were good-natured, vocally generous, ready to approve or to encourage, but when Scrimshaw called a ball that was obviously a strike, or a strike obviously a ball, their pleasure at his misperception was readily evident. "Good-eye, good-eye" was their favored response to an inept call. A blatant reversal of what was just and fair seemed to please them most.

On the ground, Starbuck sat, as near to the players' bench as protocol would allow, his legs crossed in front of him, his mouth open, his eye enlivened by fear and expectation now that Phillip was up to bat. Unlike his fellow spectators, he offered no encouragements, no praise, no assurances. His only movement was to cover his ears each time the pitch was made, a misdirected gesture obviously intended for the eyes, but diverted, in the tension of the moment, to the ears. After Scrimshaw had made the call, he would lower his hands, keeping them at the ready, like headphones through which he might receive important news.

Starbuck's great moment so far had come at the end of the first inning when Phillip had trotted in from left field and was presented, by Starbuck, with a Pepsi. In fulfillment of the inmate code, it was expected that Starbuck would ply his jock with drink for his thirst when he played for the honor and glory of the tier. Phillip easily tolerated Starbuck's presentations, not only because the young man obviously enjoyed the endless giving, but because it was yet another public proof of their hookup. Their appearances in the television room, in the yard, at meals, supported by Starbuck's eager gifts, seemed to have convinced everyone that here indeed was a valid coupling and it deserved respect.

Only McTygue, one of the guards on the tier, a lean, dog-faced man with a faint mole on his cheek suggesting German shepherd ancestry, had seemed disapproving. "I'm watching you, Manrahan. You know that, don't you? I'm lookin' at you." Or, "Don't you go making me puke, Starbuck.

Some things, they make me puke when I see them. Like you and your Daddy together. So far, okay. But don't go making me want to puke."

At first Phillip was tempted to tell McTygue that his concerns were unnecessary: he could look all he wanted, nothing would ever offend either his eyes or his digestion. Then Phillip learned—from a phrase here, an overheard remark there—that McTygue was actually voicing pleas and disappointments, not warnings. As guard of the tier, he was to report any sexual activity and turn in a 115, a disciplinary write-up, which would result in confinements and restrictions for several weeks at a time. Whatever McTygue might observe, of course, was through the windows provided in each door for just such a purpose, a random and unannounced surveillance. In the spirit of quid pro quo and tit for tat, McTygue however, had devised an arrangement of mutual satisfaction. In fulfillment of his duty, he would, from time to time, peer through the glass to make certain nothing untoward was taking place inside. If, as might happen, an inmate or two or three were having a scaled-down Saturnalia, the activity would not abruptly stop, but would continue with, perhaps, increased intensity, and McTygue, in return for not filing a 115, would be allowed to watch. Sometimes these displays were prearranged, an agreed upon bribe for other privileges. Sometimes they were required in payment for an infraction in quite another area and, as far as Phillip could tell, no one on the tier had found the arrangement other than useful and acceptable.

That he and Starbuck had provided McTygue with no such enjoyments obviously annoyed the man, and Phillip kept in mind that he and Starbuck had both better be somewhat cautious, not in their domestic displays, but in their everyday activities. One wrong move and, to avoid disciplinary retaliation, they might have to perform, for McTygue's benefit, some sexual gymnastic that would violate his and Starbuck's chaste, unsullied bond.

Phillip refused the Pepsi. He wasn't thirsty and said so. "No," Starbuck said, "you're thirsty. Drink this." His voice was neither pleading nor commanding. It was merely instructive. So Phillip took a few swigs, let the Pepsi sear down his throat. He handed the Pepsi back. "You finish it." Then, taking a cue from Starbuck's own method of persuasion, he added, "You're thirsty." Starbuck nodded, accepted the can, and, without taking a drink, went back to his place just to the right of home plate.

Now the pitcher who, in a manifestation of wit unparalleled was being called Koufax, began his warm-up, the ball held out, then brought to his chest, rubbed as if for luck, then held out again. His right leg went up, bent at the knee, and he twisted to his left as if to show Phillip his asshole.

The ball snapped out of Koufax's hand, Phillip made the swing, and it was strike two. "Go Daddy go!" Koufax repeated his gyration, offering Phillip the same view of his asshole just before releasing the ball. The pitch was good, but Scrimshaw called it ball three. "Good-eye, good-eye, good-eye." The commendation was general among his mates, deteriorating in its final moments to "Ga-die, ga-die, ga-die," the repetition now sounding like the comments of a gaggle of demented geese.

Koufax repeated his presentation, and it occurred to Phillip that what most pitchers really intended was to fart in the batter's face. The ball snapped free, and Phillip swung. The swing caught. The quick snap of wood cracked against the ball told him to drop the bat and run. Which he did. Not for all he was worth—he wanted to savor the sense of reserve strength his exercises had earned him—but with a rush and a force that got him to where he was supposed to be before the ball might arrive.

For a moment, nobody made a sound. Phillip, managing not to pant, saw Folger and Butte staring at him. Starbuck had stood up and couldn't stop blinking. Then Bowersox called out, "Daddy-did! Daddy-did!" and, to relieve the silence, the cry was taken up, accompanied by clapping and one or two whistles. Phillip was safe on first.

Dawson struck out, Lutcher struck out, and Phillip's first-base hit had been to no avail—except that it diminished everyone's good spirits. He was disappointing them. He was somewhat effective; he could catch, throw, hit, and run. His fall to one knee had provided them with the only gleeful moment so far and they were becoming if not outright hostile, at least suspicious that they'd been tricked. The opportunities for ridicule, for repeated plays on the word "Daddy" seemed not to be forthcoming. Butte, as if in warning, came up to him, gave his behind the obligatory swat and said, "Relax. It's only a game. Don't push it. Enjoy. That's what it's for. Right?" He swatted him one more time to emphasize his sincerity.

Phillip renewed his teammates' faith in him by not catching a pop fly, missing a throw to third, and falling flat out when he tried to grab a grounder down the base line. "Daddy-do" was brought back into play and the glee mounted when he dropped the ball after a stunning low catch, then reached its climax when he made a wild throw to second and hit the runner on the shoulder. "Daddy-did" competed with "Ga-die, ga-die, ga-die," as the acclaim of choice. He was beginning to reward their expectations. When he got back from the outfield, no member of the team exempted himself from the pleasure of slapping his behind in gratitude and congratulation for his ineptitude. Starbuck, ever faithful, brought him—now that he was finally thirsty—a bag of potato chips. He did it almost solemnly, impressed by his association with an actual member of an actual baseball team.

On the bench, waiting his turn at bat, Phillip dutifully ate, making as much noise as possible, crunching the salty flakes between his tongue and pallet. He owed it to Starbuck to be as loud as he could. None did he offer to his colleagues even though Folger, while Bowersox was at bat, turned toward him to watch the jaw go up and down, to hear the noisy snaps like amplified knuckle cracking. "The kid's good to you, ain't he?" Folger said, the use of "ain't" an affectation. Folger was a college graduate, given three years for paying off six jockeys and neglecting to pay off a seventh. His adoption of ungrammatical construction and what he assumed to be lower-class syntax would have been embarrassing if it hadn't been so expert. He was a superb actor. He excelled in any chosen role, this one of a cheerful but knowing convict right out of a forties movie, a character created, no doubt, by the fruitful union of Jimmy Cagney and John Garfield.

Phillip waited for Folger to say more about Starbuck's perfections. It would help recall him to his first reason for being there: to crack skulls.

But Folger, after seeming to search the side of Phillip's head for a place to settle his gaze, turned and looked out past the baseball diamond, past the handball court and the jogging track, at the high concrete wall at the far end of the yard. Determined not to look at him, Phillip took in a few more potato chips and made even louder crackling sounds to let Folger know he had no interest in what he might say.

But Folger found a way to interest him anyway.

"My spies in the records office tell me you got a sister's a nun. Next of kin they said."

Phillip gathered up the rest of the potato chips from the bottom of the bag, leaned his head back, and dropped them into his mouth. Mostly broken bits, too small to make much noise, they didn't give Phillip the sound cover he wanted, so he began crushing, crinkling the bag between his hands.

"I went to a school had nuns when I was a kid. Franciscans."

Something in the tone of Folger's voice made Phillip want to turn and look directly at him, but he settled for watching Bowersox take a swing, his first strike. Folger leaned back, his shoulders and head touching the clubhouse wall, the beak of his cap rising out from behind a shock of dark hair, more like a red tiara than the badge and emblem of a jock. His hands curled loosely around the front edge of the bench. Phillip crushed the bag a little more, then let it spring back so he could crumple it all over again.

The players from tier three, out in the field, were babbling encouragement to Koufax. The shortstop had taken off his cap and was scratching the top of his head. The man in left field was clapping his hands in anticipation of some feat not yet achieved, and the outfielder seemed to be checking the soles of his shoes for dog shit even though there were no dogs in the entire prison compound. Starbuck had upended the Pepsi can and appeared to have his nose stuck in the opening.

Phillip stopped crinkling the bag. He held it in his fist, its corners sharp, poking into the palm of his hand. The voice Folger was using seemed not to be his own. The overemphatic sincerity had been removed; it was no longer probing for points of entry where it might insinuate itself

75

among fears and weaknesses and work its usual mischief. Gone was the insolent tone of praise or the sneer of congratulation. In its place was a tentative confidentiality, like an advance scout sent into uncertain terrain to check for a friendly presence.

"Your sister, her name's Sister Rachel is what I heard."

The pitcher did his windup, the prescribed rudeness, the flung arm, the release, the throw. "Strike two!" the umpire called, raising two fingers in a victory sign. Had it been Phillip at bat, he would have connected. He would have shorn the skin from the ball and sent the naked skull arching high until it cracked and splintered the distant concrete wall. That Folger should say his sister's name was not permissible. Phillip didn't move, except for a slight tightening of his fist so that the pointed edges of the bag dug deeper into his palm, and there was the quick squeak of the cellophane being squeezed even closer into itself.

But Folger neither noticed nor heard. As far as Phillip could tell, he was still staring out at the prison wall. "I'm going to ask you a favor," Folger said, "and I hope you'll listen and that you'll understand."

This reversion to grammar, this retreat into civilized syntax only added to Phillip's anger. Folger was setting him up for some ultimate insult, some final obscenity. And it would involve his sister. Phillip considered warning him, but decided to say nothing. He would let Folger talk, let him say what he had to say. Then crack his skull.

"What I'm going to say will sound strange," Folger said, "but I'm going to say it anyway." He paused. "In the game we play next week against the college kids coming here, I've got to win. It's very important. I can't lose." He looked again at the side of Phillip's head, only now he didn't seem to be searching for a place to stop. He had already settled for Phillip's left ear. Folger was staring right into it, trying to penetrate it. Still Phillip didn't move.

"Daddy-up! Daddy-up!" The tier mates had taken up the babble and were joined by inmates from the third tier. "Daddy-up! Daddy-up!" Bowersox had made it to second on a dropped ball by the shortstop. Phillip was up.

76

Before he'd made it halfway to the plate, Folger was behind him, dusting him off, his shoulders, his back, his arms. He was saying something, very distinct, but it was barely audible beneath the brushes and slaps of the dusting. "Ask your sister to pray we win. Ask her to pray for the game with the college. We've got to win. Understand what I'm saying? We win. Or we die. Tell her my full name is Jason Folger. And she might mention Butte. Roger Butte. Junior." Again he paused, then made himself say, "Please. Nuns pray for you when you ask them. So ask, okay?"

Folger had moved around and was dusting Phillip from the front. The dusting stopped. Phillip ignored him and stepped up to the plate. "Daddy-up Daddy-up!" Whatever one's allegiance, to whichever tier, Phillip was the favorite. They were clearly counting on him to strike out, and in a spectacular and particularly ludicrous way. Maybe Folger had said what he'd said just to rattle him. To undo him. To make sure there'd be no repeat of the first-base hit.

To give himself time, Phillip employed the usual procrastinations: he tapped the bat on the plate, he sniffed, he spat, he wiggled inside his clothes, he tried a few half-swings, took off his cap, wiped his forehead with his arm, jerked his head to put his hair back in place, pulled the cap down over the hair, then stuck out his behind to let the pitcher know he was ready.

Phillip knew Folger had been trying to tell him something. The words had been in code and it was Phillip's job to decipher them. He gripped the bat tighter and held it out. The pitch came. Phillip swung. He heard the crack, like the clean split of something that managed to be both solid and hollow at the same time. Instinctively, he dropped the bat as if he'd heard a starting pistol, and began to run. There was yelling, but the first baseman was just standing there, doing nothing. Phillip, in his confusion, must have made a mistake. He must not have even hit the ball. The rush he'd felt at the cracking, the sense of vindictive glee was an emotion to which he had earned no right. The shouts were telling him to return to home plate. He saw Bowersox cross the plate for a run. Butte was shaking Bowersox's hand, but he was yelling at Phillip.

Near the bench, Starbuck was standing, his hands clamped over his mouth. Phillip's teammates had gathered around home plate, a ragged circle, slapping each other—on the arms, on the backs and, of course, on the buttocks, a kind of frisking in joyful search of who-knew-what. Only Folger had remained where he was, seated, looking at Phillip, his hands again holding onto the edge of the bench.

Phillip had hit a home run. The ball had gone into the handball court, the agreed-upon place for a homer. He continued past first, past second, where the second baseman muttered a congratulatory "Break your leg, motherfucker."

Between third and home, his run easy, Phillip tipped sideways to his right, jumped up on his left foot, and let out a stifled howl. He'd turned his ankle. When he put the foot back onto the ground, trying not to break stride, it folded under him. He stopped, his right foot lifted from the ground. He looked up at the sky, at the guard tower at the far corner of the wall. Slowly he lowered the foot to the ground.

His final steps to home plate were half-run, half-limp. His teammates were silent a moment, then came toward him, gathered around him, and accompanied him the rest of the way. He was given the slaps that were his due. Butte took him by the elbow and was leading him back to the bench next to Folger. He heard "Easy, Daddy, easy," and a weakened almost whimpered call of congratulations from the rabble: "Daddy did it. Daddy did it."

Starbuck, clearly awed by the injury, approached Phillip from the side and tentatively held out a fresh Pepsi, not sure if he were qualified to come near someone who had hit a home run and had injured himself for the sake of the tier. Phillip shook his head no. He sat down next to Folger. Folger said nothing. Phillip moved his injured ankle out in front of him. Without looking at Folger, he said, "At the college game, you're going to escape. Right? You and Butte?" When there was no answer, he lowered his head and looked down at the beaten dust in front of the bench. He wished he hadn't cracked Folger's skull and sent his head flying into the handball court.

Starbuck came and sat down next to Phillip but said nothing. He yanked open the tab of the Pepsi. A great spray shot up into his face, some of it getting onto Phillip's shoulder and into his ear. Starbuck covered the top of the can, letting the sticky foam bubble out over his fingers.

"You hit yourself a home run," he said quietly.

"Yeah."

"You hurt your foot."

"Ankle."

"You hurt your ankle."

"Yeah."

Starbuck took his hand from the top of the Pepsi and, reaching over, put his arm across Phillip's back, curling his wet fingers around his left arm. Then he lay his head against Phillip's shoulder and, after a moment, took a long deep gulp of the Pepsi, then another. Phillip could hear the Pepsi fizzing its way down Starbuck's throat. He decided not to move.

FIVE

Rachel stepped away from the painting, lifted her head higher, then cocked it to the right. She was almost finished, but couldn't make up her mind if she should put halos around the heads. At the Last Supper, they weren't saints—not yet—which meant no halos. But she wasn't painting the meal as it was, but a memorial to the meal, an artistic celebration of the historic event. They were saints now, at this time of the painting—which argued for halos. Ordinarily, she'd also have to make the decision about Judas. Orthodoxy hardly allotted him a halo—even though, without him, the redemptive betrayal and crucifixion would presumably not have taken place. But this particular contribution cut little ice—as a matter of fact, it cut no ice at all with those forever on the lookout for the unforgivable sin. Judas was hardly Rachel's hero, but she'd often had the nagging suspicion that he'd gotten bad press. And besides, those who insisted on his damnation—the solemn, the righteous, the smug—were themselves tempting hellfire for their belief that God's grace lacked the ferocity needed to overwhelm even this arch villain of history. Rachel's solution to the Iscariot quandary had been to simply not include him in the picture to begin with. This was, after all, her version of the

Passover meal and, as an artist, she could do whatever was consistent with her own vision. Her vision did not include a villain of any kind.

This still left her with her first question: halos or no halos. No halos, she thought; she had no gold paint. But then, she did have yellow, a nice bright yellow, and Mother had complained, on the evidence of her smock, about her not having used enough yellow. This certainly weighed heavily in the scales. She reached for the tube of yellow. If she'd hold it in her hand, maybe squeeze it a little, it would help her decide. But before she could pick out the yellow tube from among the heap that cluttered the refectory serving table, she heard through the pantry door three "pings," the high-pitched sound that meant Mother wanted something.

That it had been three pings meant Rachel had no need to hurry. The number of pings determined the haste with which she was to answer a summons. At first, Mother had thought that a repeated number of pings, with their implicit panic, would indicate emergency, but then reasoned that, in a real crisis, she might not have the strength for more than one push of the pearl-colored button that would sound the necessary ping in the pantry downstairs. So it was decided: three pings meant Rachel could take her time; two pings meant come at once; one ping meant she was already too late.

This ancient means of summoning servants, a remnant of the mansion's earlier days, had been reinstituted when the Mother General had become sick, and Rachel rather liked participating in an activity that recalled the days of power and worldly magnificence. Now when she'd answer Mother's ping, she would bustle up the stairs, maybe wiping her hands on her apron or smock, curious as to the cause for the summons, eager to be drawn into the larger extravagance that was the life of the house itself.

That Rachel had been cast as servant bothered her not at all; that she'd been given any role whatsoever was sufficient in itself, letting her imagination, at the sound of the ping, create an immigrant girl, young, impatient, good-humored, with a flourishing head of auburn hair that waved and curled in unmanageable profusion. She would mutter her complaints about overwork and the general foolishness of the rich, speaking in a lilting brogue. She was named, more often than not, Brigid. "Surely" would be Brigid's most favored word: "Surely you'll want this," "Surely you won't want that," "Surely, if that's what you'd like," "Surely I got here as quick as I could." A good soul, Brigid, faithful, impertinent, sly, with a heart as big as a house, as fine a character as ever inhabited a play by a playwright given to cliché and to obvious dramaturgy. But, pity to tell, poor Brigid, whose part was small enough to begin with, never survived when her hand would reach up to touch her auburn profusion and discover, in place of its curls and locks, the short ill-combed hair of Sister Rachel, who spoke with a somewhat flattened lilt and knew only too well that she was neither sly nor impertinent and would never marry the butcher's boy as Brigid would have done, surely.

Rachel quickly picked up the tube of yellow and squirted a small dab of the paint onto the palm of her hand. After she'd replaced the cap and put the tube down, she rubbed her hands together as if applying lotion, then wiped them on the upper left corner of her smock just below the collarbone. Even if she hadn't made up her mind about halos or no halos, she could at least give Mother the satisfaction of seeing a smock on which yellow was minimally represented.

After she'd cleaned her hands with turpentine, locked the refectory door behind her—no one was allowed in before the painting was finished—she stopped in the kitchen, washed her hands, wiped them again on the sides of her smock and, more with her own somewhat angular step than with Brigid's supple and eager bustle, started across the vast empty expanse of the great hall.

Her feet were bare, as usual. She thought it more economical to clean the paint off her feet than to apply turpentine again and again to her shoes, cracking the leather, rotting the stitch. The linoleum felt cool and clean. The expensive rugs and thick-piled carpets had disappeared long ago, and, lately, most of the furniture as well. When the mansion was first bequeathed to the Order at the turn of the twentieth century the then Mother General, Sister Adelaide, had accepted the donation, but with misgivings. The huge stone house, with two towers, a conservatory, an entrance hall the size of a tennis court, and a stately staircase leading not just to a landing but to a stained-glass window that seemed appropriated from Chartres, was considered far too opulent for a community of women who had renounced the wealth of the world. True, the stained glass suggested a churchly motif, but the general grandeur seemed a contradiction. True, they—the nuns—would still live in basic poverty, accepting no more than their simplest needs—food, clothing, shelter— but there was no avoiding, no denying that, according to appearances, they would be living pretty high on the hog. In its own way, it shamed them to live in a mansion.

It was the word "shame" to which Sister Adelaide attached her acceptance. In humility, they would accept the house and bear the shame. The house would be a constant reminder of what they had renounced; they would be surrounded by accusing opulence; they would inhabit contradiction, never forgetting, as they took each step through the wide corridors, descended the magnificent staircase, gathered together in the paneled rooms, sat in the heavy carved chairs at the finely crafted table, or sank into the pillowed couches, that this was the extreme, the ultimate declaration of what they had surrendered.

Most of the sisters came from clapboard houses, overcrowded with unruly brothers and sisters, shared beds and one bathroom, unkempt yards whose greatest glory was a stand of hollyhocks and maybe a few stubborn sunflowers. What the mansion told them, day in, day out, was that where they were living was not their home. They had no home. They had only this heap of stone, this expanse of polished wood and gilded plaster, this monument to money, and they must be satisfied for the simple reason that it offered shelter—and they needed shelter if they were going to be able to do the work they'd been called to do. It also allowed the donor to make his gift, which had been a heartfelt act that could not be dismissed or scorned. A rich man, too, has a soul to save, or so they'd been taught to believe. In charity the house had been given, in charity it had been accepted, and that, said Sister Adelaide, was that.

Sister Adelaide did, however, insist on one concession. All the rare and figured rugs, vast carpets of intricate design and welcoming colors, the plush pile comforting even the most weary or ague-plagued foot, they all had to go. They were sold, auctioned, the proceeds put into the general coffers. And in their stead was installed that glowing, shining symbol of hardworking respectability, linoleum. Its very glare cried out "scrubwoman," its unspotted shine reflected more readily than anything else the kneeling, sweating servant. They were in the mansion, but they were not of the mansion, just as they were in the world, but not of the world. They awoke to this reminder, they lived within it, and when sleep came, they knew themselves to be objects of charity, submissive even to contradiction. And should they forget in some opulent dream their chosen state, the first step onto the morning linoleum brought them back hastily to the glory and the drudgery known only to those who have nothing they can call their own.

When Rachel reached the foot of the staircase, she stopped and looked at the alarm clock on the spindly table near the vestibule to the main door. She could hear the ticking. It seemed to be running all right, but she decided not to take any chances. It had replaced the grandfather clock that had stood sentry, as they say, for years beyond memory. Its solemn tock had been considerably louder than the tick of its successor; its chimes gentle, more a soft, surprised comment on the passing of time than the tolling of time gone. The whirr and grind of gears before the hours were struck had seemed the gruff introduction of an impatient husband who then left the actual statement to be delivered by a sweet and amiable wife, her tones touching the air rather than sounding through it, tender, almost apologetic for the intrusion.

The old clock, of course, had been sold, but not as an act of renunciation. It was a practical matter that went beyond the need for money. Because the Motherhouse was being closed for good and forever, piece by piece, sometimes room by room, the furniture had been sold, the money given to the diocese, which, for some time now, had taken on the financial dealings of the Order. The resident nuns—Mother General and Sister Rachel included—were not being robbed of their goods and chattel, nor was the mansion itself being stripped of what glories had survived the near century of monastic occupation. The real reason was that the Order of the Sisters of the Annunciation was itself being dissolved. One by one its schools had closed or been absorbed into other institutions; its convents, near empty, were abandoned, each when its time came. The wide range of the Order's reach narrowed, lessened, withdrew—slowly at first, then more quickly until this present moment when, like the last survivors who had retreated under siege into the castle keep for their final stand, seven nuns, the youngest a vigorous fifty-four, kept vigil over the last days of the once flourishing and powerful community.

It was because the mansion was soon to be destroyed that Sister Rachel had been given the Mother General's permission to paint the Last Supper on the refectory wall. The painting's predetermined destruction was a condition of its creation. Rachel understood this. Like any true artist she knew that, for her, the moments of creation were all that really mattered. The days on which the work was actually done were the good days, the days of joy and thanks. The final disposition was unimportant; she accepted whatever fate might be its lasting portion. Of course, she wanted the painting to be appreciated and understood and praised, but it was not as an artist that she asked for these things. It was as the artist's representative. The artist herself would have gone off, disappeared into the work, leaving behind this insatiable surrogate, responsible for collecting accolades, condemnations, scorns, and shrugs. That Rachel, because of the painting's imminent destruction, would never be called upon to fulfill this particular role was a disappointment she accepted with the same ready sadness with which she accepted all other deprivations that defined her Sisterly state. She had asked at her investiture that she *do* more than *be*—and she'd been taken at her word.

Now the time remaining in the Motherhouse was numbered by the days allotted to the Mother General on this earth. Her death would signal that all was over. The dispersal of the final six, a shabby diaspora, would then take place: Sister Felicity, the vigorous fifty-four year old, to the Southwest to be an itinerant pastoral assistant serving the unpriested parishes in the hundreds of miles of mountain and desert territory; Sister Martha to throw in her lot with the Franciscans who ran a shelter and a soup kitchen in another town; Sister Angela to the mercy of her aging niece's family where she would live out her arthritic retirement; Sister Cathrael to the Chancery to be taught, at seventy-three, the ways of the office computers; and Sister Agatha to a slum apartment where she'd live with two Notre Dames and an Ursuline and do whatever she could for the surrounding turf. Sister Rachel would go to the bishop's residence, an addition to the housekeeping staff. And Sister Gabriel, the Mother General, would, of course, go obediently to the grave from which she would rise on the latter day.

Rachel picked up the alarm clock and, in reflex, shook it clockwise and counterclockwise, then put it to her ear even though its tick had been clearly audible all along. She lived with the certainty that the clock was unreliable and needed this kind of attention to keep it running. Convinced that it required no special correction, she wound it up with two turns of the key. (Everyone going in or out of the main door, up the stairs or down the stairs, took a moment to shake and wind the clock. It was the most cared-for clock in the world, each of its keepers convinced that she and she alone was its true and most capable guardian.) For good measure, Rachel gave the clock one more clockwise and counterclockwise turn— then put it down and started up the stairs, hiking her smock a little, an atavistic gesture recalling the days of the old voluminous garb.

When she reached the third step, a thought came to her. It made her stop. She touched the banister to steady herself. She instinctively touched her forehead to see if she had a fever. She did not. But the thought was still there, swelling inside of her, and there seemed to be nothing she could do to stop it. She would not go into service at the bishop's residence. She would not search out on the shining floors the hardened dirt in the hidden cracks and the secret corners; she would not scrape and scour along the baseboards nor would she scrub the steps or polish the floors. The bishop's tables and shelves must go undusted, his books, lamps, and paintings would

87

lie undisturbed beneath whatever siftings the air might bring. She would make no fierce rubbings of the sideboard or mantel to make them gleam. The bishop would have to look after himself.

Rachel would, when her brother had served out his sentence, go to him and look after him. He'd lost the small but handsome house in the growing suburb of their hometown that he'd bought a few years before his arrest, the money confiscated to pay back his known embezzlement. He'd need help of some kind. Not that she would become his char. Such an imposition, she knew, would never be tolerated. Besides, that wasn't what she had in mind. She would get a job. She would hire herself out for pay, and the money would go to help her brother. If no one would trust him after all his thieving, she would support the two of them. If he found work, fine; if not, there would always be her weekly wage. And if he refused, she would hit him on the side of his head. Not for a single minute would she put up with his pride—or his stubbornness either.

Rachel's bare feet stuck slightly to the cold linoleum of the stair treads, but nothing would stop her now. She continued up the steps. The suspicion that this was a new madness about to overwhelm her brought its own terrors; she could feel it quickening in her throat; it could become a laugh or a scream. But she swallowed hard and kept going. She must not be afraid; she must not despair. This was a new and truthful calling. She must surrender her old and beloved vows; she must accept humbly and with a full spirit this latest summons, and give thanks. The thoughts were now tumbling joyfully inside of her, growing, irresistible. To the Mother General she would reveal her calling and from Mother herself she would receive the required dispensation, the needed benediction. Together they would weep with gratitude for this divine revelation, then smile at the foolishness of their tears.

Rachel had passed the landing and had reached the top of the stairs. She paused and looked down at her feet. Big oversized feet, they would humble her and make her calm. Smudges of brown and yellow gave her left foot a sickly appearance; her right foot had obviously come down with the chicken pox. But enough green was strewn in among the pox to make the foot seem somewhat festive. Her feet were still too big. She came quickly to an old acceptance dating back to her novitiate when she had given up the lifelong embarrassment of having big feet, asking that, in exchange, she be given a calming humility at the mere sight of them. It wasn't just the threat of vanity that her feet would overcome: they could arrest the onslaught of enthusiasm, or an excess of exhilaration. They were doing it now; anyone with feet this big had no right to be giddy. Anyone planted so firmly on the ground should realize that she had been destined for the practical and the levelheaded. She had not been intended for ecstasy; she should be, quite literally, down-to-earth.

And her new determination about her brother was practical. It made all the sense in the world. That she should be visited with so clear a vision, so obvious an idea, was the source of her delight. It was not her madness come again. Its simplicity was what had thrilled her; its absolute rightness had inspired her rapture.

Rachel felt again the stirrings not only of this newfound joy, but she seemed to feel, as well, an old assurance, an assurance long since lost. This, too, worried her. She wasn't used to feeling this way; it all belonged to the Rachel she had been before her cure. That certainty might come again—that it might even be there, inside her now, rushing through her whole body, made her both terrified and serene at the same time. She would let happen what seemed to be happening. She would not resist. Big feet or not, she would experience the elation she'd been trying to calm. But she would, at the same time, insist again: her idea was practical.

She smoothed her smock, fluffed her short unruly hair, and knocked on Mother's door. No one answered. She knocked again. Still no answer. She knocked harder.

"Yes, come in." It was Mother's voice, but muffled, as if she had her hand over her mouth. Rachel opened the door. Mother was out of bed, standing at the windows, facing the river. Her right hand was resting on the sill; other than this, nothing steadied or supported her. She did not turn around. Rachel was too surprised to say anything but the obvious: "Mother! You're out of bed!"

The fingers of Mother's right hand diddled lightly on the sill as if she were playing a piece by Chopin. Rachel started across the room, stopped halfway, then went back and closed the door. It was, for no reason Rachel could explain, unseemly that Mother should be out of bed unassisted. No one else must see, even though Mother was clothed from throat to ankle by a white flannel nightgown. Rachel crossed the room in a flurry, rather like a meteorological disturbance, creating quick displacements of air, slight stirrings of unsecured objects as far from her as the dresser along the wall and the night table near the bed. She repeatedly reached out her hands, anxious to give support, but afraid to annoy the forces that had agreed to allow Mother to stand unaided at the window.

Rachel's mouth moved, not to say anything or even to make a sound, but to prepare the lips for whatever words they might soon have to deliver. Even when she reached Mother's side, she was reluctant to take hold of her. One did not, after all, go grabbing at the Mother General. Twice Rachel's arm twitched in Mother's direction, the hand lifting slightly, only to be dropped again at her side. Rather than interrupt Mother at what she might be doing, Rachel simply stood at her side, ready for whatever might happen.

Mother was smiling, but it was a hard smile. It had compressed rather than loosened her lips, and it had drawn her eyes back deeper into her head. Her flesh, which had seemed taut, alert, was relaxed, as if it had released the bones from their responsibility to give it shape. She stood as erect as her bent spine might allow, the hump between her shoulders thrusting her head forward, her curved vertebrae providing her with a stance of eagerness, the appearance of an almost benevolent, buzzardlike delight in what she was seeing.

"Aren't your feet cold?" Rachel asked.

"I don't know. They're too numb for me to tell if they're hot or cold."

"Maybe Mother would like to get back into bed."

"Mother would like to look out the window for just a few more minutes. Then you can do whatever you like with her."

Rachel managed not to glance around the room, to see where

Mother's bathrobe might be, or her slippers. She looked out at the lawn, straw-colored and overgrown, and at the two tattered oleander bushes, one on each side of the front door. Her gaze reached the driveway and followed its curve toward the slope of the hill where it disappeared in among the trees, pine mostly, with a maple and an oak here and there and a birch or two deep within. This forced her to raise her eyes to see, down past the curve of the roadway and the forested hillside, the dark green of shaded leaves, the river itself, slowly moving, then the shoe factory.

"Father Laughlin won't be coming to say Mass," Mother said. "He has one of his colds and shouldn't come near me."

Rachel nodded her head with understanding. Father Laughlin had been having colds and fevers all summer, and there had been more days than Rachel could name when the elderly priest had had to send word that he wouldn't be able to be there. And with only Father Kilbara with him at St. Joseph's, and Father Kilbara running two parishes—St. Joan of Arc as well—there was no one to send in Father Laughlin's place. "I'll go to the chapel then," Rachel said, "and bring you communion."

"In a minute."

"Shall I help you back into bed?"

Mother didn't answer. She tried to raise her head but succeeded only in tipping it sideways, away from Rachel. Mother reached her left hand out, toward the window, but quickly put it back onto the sill to help keep her balance. "Tell me," she said, "is it, what you see out there, is it beautiful?"

"Yes."

"Very beautiful?"

"Yes. Very beautiful."

Gravely Mother nodded her head, not in agreement but in acceptance. "And do you love it, what you see?"

"Love it?"

"Yes. Love it."

Rachel looked at Mother's profile, the slant of the nose a continuation of the line of the forehead, the wet lips, the failed chin. When the lips began to tremble, Rachel turned back to look out the window.

"Well?" Mother said.

"Yes," Rachel said. "I love it."

Again Mother nodded her acceptance. "Tell me, what does it feel like, this love you have."

"But Mother knows what it feels like."

"Mother does not know what it feels like. If Mother knew, Mother wouldn't ask."

"But—"

"What does it feel like? Please tell me. If you can."

Rachel dug her hands deep into her smock pockets and lowered her head. She noticed she hadn't dusted the windowsill. There were streaks and smudges where Mother had put her fingers—as if small animals had been romping around under the impression that the accumulated dust was really a light fall of snow.

"Well?" Mother's fingers twiddled again on the sill, creating in the dust new evidence of play.

"Well," Rachel said quietly, looking down as if ashamed, "it's a feeling, a presence—inside of me—and it starts in my stomach." Rachel now raised her head and looked out. "Yes. I'm looking out the window at what we see, and there it is, this feeling in my stomach. And now it's going up into my chest—wait—it's going outward too, into my fingers. I can feel it in my fingers and—and, yes, my toes. It's come into my toes! And into my head, pressing a little against the inside of my skull. It's all over me now. It's in my ears, my cheeks, it's behind my eyes; it's all the way through me. See? I have to open my mouth, to let my chin down, to let some of the feeling out, because there's so much of it. I love it. It's all through me, everywhere. Everything out there is inside me now because I love it."

"Ah," Mother said. "It begins in the stomach?"

"Yes, Mother. For me it does."

For a moment, neither of them stirred. Then Rachel said, "Now maybe Mother should let me help her back into bed."

Mother shook her head. "I envy you. Deeply. I came here to the window to give one last look. Outside. At the world you find so beautiful. I took a terrible chance, but I needn't have worried. I wanted to see if now I could, at the end, just before I die, if I could love the world spread out there before me. I have looked. And I don't love it. I have been spared. It would have been devastating if I did. The regret that the love should come so late, that the beauty should be seen and recognized now, at the moment of parting, would have been unbearable. I would have died in torment. I took the chance. I gambled, and I won. I look out now at everything you see. But I feel nothing. I don't love it. It's just there. To think—the created world, the handiwork of God, the delight of his eye, I've seen it—but what is it to me!" She leaned forward until her forehead and the ridge of her nose touched the window. Her eyes were closed, her knuckles pressed down onto the sill. She moved her head from side to side as if trying to grind something into the glass. "I don't love it." She whispered, as if denying something she knew to be true. With her left hand, she reached over toward Rachel, unsteady, clawing at the sleeve of the smock.

Rachel moved closer and Mother grabbed her arm, bunching the sleeve into her grip, pinching the muscle beneath. Mother moved back from the window, her head bent low, a continuation of the humped spine. Her words were muffled again, with a slight lisp at the edges, her voice a hoarse whisper. "This is my last confession. I have not loved the world. I have loved serving it, and that must be enough. Now, you may bring me communion."

"Yes, Mother." Rachel took the old woman's arm just below the elbow and helped turn her away from the window. Mother took a step toward the bed, but stopped. "Quickly," she said. "Quickly. I can't feel the floor. I don't know where it is." She tried to take a second step, but her body began to crumple, the knees first, then the spine. Rachel put her left hand across Mother's back, held it there, then slowly reached down her right hand and raised the humped, light-boned body into her arms.

Mother opened her mouth, and Rachel readied herself for the command to put her back down, but instead, Mother began to laugh, a gargling in the back of her throat. "I'm being carried!" she called out. "I'm floating right through the air."

Rachel placed her on the bed, making sure the head was at the center of the three pillows necessary to accommodate the bent spine. She pulled the blanket out from under the legs, then brought it up and placed it gently just below the throat. Mother hiccuped, then made the gargling sound, but more softly. As Rachel went out of the room to get the Eucharist, she heard Mother whispering, "I have been lifted up. . . ."

It was when Rachel was walking back through the great hall, the bread carried like a rescued bird between her cupped hands, that the doorbell rang. She continued across the hall. Maybe Sister Martha would answer. Rachel started toward the staircase. The bell rang again, more insistent. Rachel was afraid the sound might disturb Mother. She moved toward the kitchen to see if she could find Sister Martha. When the bell rang again, Rachel looked through the frosted glass into the small outer vestibule. The bell rang, even as she looked, a high-pitched warning, the sound an urgent alarm. Two men were outside, one carrying what looked like a suitcase on his shoulder. The one without the suitcase had seen her shape through the blur of the translucent glass and was waving. Because of the frosted glass, it always seemed to Rachel, even on the hottest day, that those at the door were being left to stand in the cold, that they'd be freezing. To bring the two men in out of the weather, Rachel, her left hand closed over the bread, opened first the vestibule door, then the door to the outside.

One of the men asked to see Sister Rachel Manrahan. Rachel asked them in and told the man she was Sister Rachel Manrahan. The other man, the one who hadn't spoken, wasn't really carrying a suitcase after all. It looked like a large musical instrument of some kind, with a black horn pointing outward. The man pointed the horn at Rachel. More words were spoken, but Rachel didn't seem to know their meaning. All she knew was that, with his words, it was as though the man had lashed her across the face with a whip. After she had cried out, she looked again at the man. Again he lashed the whip across her face, forcing her head far to the side, the pain catching her in the throat, in the back of the skull. To make the man stop, she pleaded, her voice a whisper, "Please. I am carrying the body of Christ. I mustn't speak."

That evening on the television news, pictures were shown of a woman in a paint-smudged smock standing at the foot of a huge staircase, a great stained-glass window above at the landing. Her hands were cupped one over the other. An unseen voice asked her if she was Sister Rachel Manrahan. The woman, puzzled, admitted that she was. The unseen voice then informed her that her brother, Phillip Manrahan, in prison for embezzlement, had murdered a prison guard. The woman had jerked her head aside. The unseen voice then informed her that, by state law, her brother would be executed for the crime, in the electric chair. Again the woman quickly thrust her face away. When asked to comment on the information, she said, "Please. I am carrying the body of Christ. I mustn't speak."

The woman then turned and went up the broad staircase toward the stained-glass window. The camera, following, showed that the woman's feet were bare and smudged with paint, one mostly brown, the other green and red.

SIX

Everything was white. The walls were white, the ceiling was white, the bars of his cell were white. Even the floor was white. Phillip had expected dingy gray, the hard metal dusted not with rust but with a black graphite that would have forced its way from the core of the iron to the surface. He had expected cement floors like the worn sidewalks of a slum neighborhood, and the exaggerated echo of every sound as if each word, each step, each motion and gesture were coming to him from a great and empty distance. He had been certain that the lights would be as dim as dishwater and that his cell would have a slop bucket instead of a toilet, with chemical fumes that would sear the nose and blunt the breath. If he hadn't exactly expected the bread of sorrow and the water of affliction, he had thought at least of grudging meals, ill-prepared, turnips—mashed—or a soup made of melted lard and, of course, more turnips.

Phillip had to admit that he had designed for himself a setting that had been heavily influenced by films, by television, and by Dostoevsky. Although Death Row was indeed a "row"—twelve cells in a line, facing a blank white wall—little else complied with preconceived images. True, he had been brought in hobbled by leg irons, his hands cuffed behind him, his pants unbelted, and his shirt a little short in the sleeves, but when the three guards, nameless, cheerful to each other and casual to him, brought him through the second security door, he felt he had been released into a medical facility, a laboratory where quiet and important experiments were being conducted.

Brightly lit, the prison was a near-shadowless country, sterile and efficient. The walls seemed not to have been painted, but rather to have had the white enamel baked right on so they could be neither chipped nor carved. In the corridor, as in the medium-security prison in which he'd murdered the guard, McTygue, there was a desk crowded with technical apparatus of computerlike design, the least of which was a telephone complex (white) that made it all seem the impressive outpost of some command station that monitored the great experiments underway.

The man seated behind the desk was, when they came into the corridor, busy with the computer, not looking up at them, but watching, it seemed, their every move on a screen to the right of a keyboard that suggested the organ in the loft of St. Aloysius where he'd served as an altar boy. The guard at the desk paused in his performance only long enough to put on his uniform cap, which had been sheltering an oblong silver box, like a tea cozy covering a teapot. Now that he was in full uniform, his performance gained momentum—*con brio*—and the cell door slid open, almost soundless, a pneumatic release of air, polite, subdued, like the opening of the door to a bus. The guard pulled a short lever and pushed two more computer keys, verifying the importance of what he'd already done.

The man himself was white-haired and red-faced, with the snub nose that Phillip always associated with a stubby dick. For all his maneuvers and manipulations the man apparently got little exercise: he was thick rather than fat, somewhat cylindrical, like a squat column. If it weren't for his arms breaking the vertical lines, he would have looked like a stump pedestal with a head displayed on top. The man made a quick run of his fingers along a set of keys and gave the screen a closer scrutiny.

Then, with his index finger, he poked a single button three times as if ending a musical composition in the same key in which it had begun.

As Phillip was put into his cell, he felt quite keenly that he was there as part of the research for which all these elaborate mechanisms had been devised. He was a guinea pig, a rabbit, a monkey, being put into its cage to await the pleasure and the need of those doing the scientific explorations. He was there to be experimented upon, his fate unimportant in itself, his value to be judged solely by what might be the outcome of the testing now made possible by his arrival.

The events leading up to McTygue's murder could be traced to the day Phillip hit his home run. It was then that Folger had hinted—unmistakably—at the escape attempt, by asking for prayers from Aggie. The next step was the college game itself. That afternoon, a Saturday, Phillip went to the prison library. He didn't want to be anywhere near the escape attempt—if Folger and Butte were still considering it. He told Starbuck to go to the game without him. Phillip would not be playing because of his injured ankle. Then Starbuck could tell him all about it later. Starbuck, somewhat awed that he'd been promoted to sports reporter, assured Phillip with quiet self-important nods that he would not fail in the task. Phillip had let him wear his cap, the red one given to him when he'd played that one time for the tier team. Now everyone at the game would know that Starbuck, by the cap he wore, was associated with baseball in some very intimate way. Starbuck, accepting the cap, was solemn—staring eyes, open mouth—as if he'd been entrusted with the honor of the realm. After clearing his throat and coughing twice, he indicated that his report would be worthy of the distinction so generously bestowed.

Phillip had been only half-honest with himself by going to the library to avoid the game. The library windows, at the southeast corner of the prison, looked out over both the yard and, from the other side of the room, past the stacks, out to the countryside beyond. Anytime Phillip might want to, he could simply go to the windows near the librarian's desk and see what was happening in the yard.

When he looked now, the game had already started. He could see that the bleachers, put up two days before along the first-base line, were filled with what looked like a rabble preparing to storm the Bastille. People were on their feet more often than they sat, and, for a baseball game, they were more excited than reflective. Caps were waved, whistles were tested until brought to perfect pitch, advice was shouted, with every spectator convinced that he was designated coach for the afternoon.

The warden, the aptly named Mr. Waller, was evident by his white shirt and his enviable position in the front row of a cluster of folding chairs just off first base. With him were the prison officials of rank and, of course, representatives of the college. The man in a cream-colored linen suit would be the dean, with the president, like the warden, coatless for the occasion, also in a white shirt, the sleeves rolled to the elbow. What further distinguished the warden and the college president were the caps they dutifully wore: red for the prison, because both the T-shirts and caps had been donated by Häagen-Dazs ice cream, and a dull gold for the college, possibly because one of its early benefactors had made his money in the manufacture of mustard.

A portable blackboard had been brought from one of the classrooms to serve as a scoreboard, but the chalk marks were too light to be seen from a distance. Phillip had some sense that the game was into its third inning, with the college at bat. One man was on second. Folger was playing third base, Butte in right field, and a lanky man Phillip thought he recognized from the fourth tier, Yazzetti, was pitching. Yazzetti had also been in Phillip's tailoring class, and his beef, he'd heard, had something to do with selling faulty storm windows. Phillip waited for the pitch. It was a slider, dipping just before it passed the box and the batter bought it, taking a swing that almost brought the bat up against the side of his neck. There were cheers, whistles, calls, all sent forth in a volume usually reserved for a run. Next came a curve and the batter, wiser, let it go by. Even from the distance, Phillip could hear "Good-eye! Good-eye!"

He looked for Starbuck but couldn't find him. Then, just as he turned away from the window, he caught in the corner of his eye a figure seated in the second row from the top of the stand. Starbuck was leaning forward, his elbows on his knees, his chin held in his hands, the visor of his cap pulled low. He looked like he was sitting on the toilet. When the batter took another swing, a third strike, those around Starbuck stood up to cheer the batter's insufficiency while Starbuck just lifted his chin from his hands, lowering his arms and sitting up straight. When the enthusiasts sat down again he leaned forward and, in general, resumed his toilet position. Phillip assumed he was concentrating, too serious in his reporter's assignment to engage in frivolities like cheering, jeering, or all the other desperations demanded of even the least ardent spectator.

Phillip went back to his magazine. Because so many of the inmates were at the game, the prison's most popular periodical, *Consumer Reports*, had been there on the rack and Phillip took full advantage of his luck. He, too, must concentrate. He must not give too much thought to the game. He would depend on the comparisons set down in *Consumer Reports* to keep him away from the windows. He did not want to see the escape—even though he did want, very much, to see it.

He checked out the ratings on small sporty cars. While he was reading that the manual transmission of the Saturn SC shifted fairly well, there was a sudden shout from below. What distinguished it was the absence of whistles. It didn't seem a cheer. It sounded more like a surprise. Phillip continued to read. He found out that the Saturn's clutch sometimes engaged too abruptly. The noise outside calmed itself into the equivalent of a boisterous conversation, everyone talking with angry conviction and no one listening. Phillip read on, discovering that the Saturn's engine rode stiffly, and it buzzed when revved up.

He ignored the intermittent excitements from below. He had the Toyota Paseo to consider. The Toyota's trunk, according to *Consumer Reports*, could accommodate two Pullman cases and two weekend bags. If you folded the rear seat down, you could put in a collapsed wheelchair. A prolonged shout from the yard, complete with whistles and the sound of feet stomping on wood, assured Phillip that nothing was happening except repeated attempts at decapitation and skull-cracking. None of this had anything to do with him. He would miss neither Folger nor Butte. With the two of them gone, perhaps he would no longer have to continue his biker-punk relationship with Starbuck. He could dump the kid. He would be rid of him and all his foolish solemnities. Phillip had, after all, cooperated with Starbuck not for the young man's protection, but to confront Butte and Folger, to restrict their territory by placing Starbuck beyond their reach. His pleasures hardly derived from the candy bars, Pepsis, and potato chips showered on him by his kid. Small delight it was to have Starbuck forever at his side, leaning his head against his shoulder, or making profound pronouncements into his ear: "Folger doesn't know he shouldn't wear green. Not with those eyes." Or "They don't really know how to make eggs. They should let me." With no Butte or Folger to thwart, the Starbuck show would be over. Phillip, like the two potential escapees, would be free.

Another shout went up, too soon after the one that had gone before. Baseball didn't move that fast. Phillip went to the windows. Diggins and Seligson from the second tier were there at another of the library's windows, laughing. Seligson was punching Diggins' arm. Diggins was saying "shit" with the long drawl borrowed from blacks. Dawson, Seligson explained, had stolen third, but Bowersox, going for home, was tagged and the team retired.

Out on the field the obligatory high-fives were exchanged between the teams as they passed each other on the field. Folger, heading out to left field, was obviously trying with this brotherly greeting to bend back each wrist to at least the spraining if not the breaking point. Phillip saw the college pitcher loosely shake his hand afterward as if he needed to restore it to health, and the second baseman, obviously more experienced, kept both hands behind him and accepted instead Folger's fraternal punch on his right shoulder.

Starbuck he spotted in line at the canteen. The Pepsi can at his lips was tilted upward, his head drawn back. It looked like he was trying to observe the heavens, the Pepsi his telescope. He was, no doubt, in line in anticipation of finishing his drink, making sure that he'd have a replacement of some sort—a candy bar, popcorn, potato chips—by the time the last drop had passed his lips. For Starbuck, a game was an exercise in digestion. A sports event was, to him, an opportunity to explore to the fullest the consumer's capacity to consume. A game unaccompanied by chewing, gulping and swallowing was a song without music. For Starbuck it was the flow of digestive juices that urged a game forward. Otherwise the contest would wither and die. Now at the head of the line, Starbuck was only doing his part to keep the game going. From the distance, Phillip thought he saw the flash of yet another Pepsi can, plus, in Starbuck's other hand, the white gleam that indicated a bag of popcorn. The game could now go on, it's fueling assured, and Phillip could return to *Consumer Reports*.

Having decided he'd pick a Mazda MX-3 GS over the Nissan NX2000 and the Saturn SC, for no other reason than that it wasn't the magazine's first choice, Phillip took up the subject of air conditioners. He felt smug to notice that the Friedrich (SQO6H1OA) he had installed in his bedroom four years ago was rated highest, but disappointed to see that the Emerson Quiet Cool (6DC533-A) was a superior energy saver. As if he were to go to market the next day, he read all that was written about moisture removal, thermostat performance, distribution, direction of breeze, and venting in general. He studied installation advantages, moisture drips, and noise levels. The chart absorbed him completely; he was able, with diminishing effort, to ignore the shouts and cries from below, even when, at one point, they were so prolonged that Phillip had to wonder if a prison riot were in the making.

Or was it the escape? To make sure no one grabbed the magazine while he was at the window, Phillip took it with him. Halfway there, he heard the noise stop except for a few scattered shouts. He paused, considered, then went back to his chair near the opposite wall, next to a window facing out over the countryside. He looked for a moment at the prison outbuildings, the power plant, the laundry, the gatehouse, the parking lot and, in the distance, beyond the prison walls, the two-steepled town of Chevaren that gave the prison its name. The town was perfectly placed on a small rise in the middle of the horizon.

The sun was glancing off something on top of one of the steeples like a coded message being sent to a watchful spy. The corn in the intervening fields between the prison and the town was well within the expectations of the old saying: high as your thigh by the Fourth of July. Some alfalfa was being cut by a woman on an orange tractor. She had blond hair and should be wearing a hat. On the highway, only one truck and four cars were headed east; going west were a truck hauling freight containers, a pickup with a dog in back, and what looked like his Mazda from *Consumer Reports*, red, and going over the speed limit.

The parking lot between the prison gate and the power station was more than half-filled, with two orange school buses nearest the gate. A dark blue Honda Prelude was pulling into a space about twenty feet in front of the buses. A gray Corolla was moving out near the power station, almost clipping a tan Cressada with its rear bumper.

A quick burst of cheering made him look toward the windows opposite. Without moving he listened for other shouts, other cries. After a few seconds they came, along with whistles and stompings. If his timing of the cheers was accurate, it was a second-base hit or a run from second. Seligman and Diggins had left the library. The trustee librarian, a bond salesman from the fourth tier, was punching computer keys, studying the screen, punching some more. No one else was there. The only sound was the light click of the man's fingernails against the computer keys and the grind of the orange tractor far off in the distance.

Another great cheer came up with whistles and stomping, louder than before. Phillip crossed to the window near the desk. On the field, the game was over. The two teams were slapping, punching, shaking each other's hands in a last attempt to maim. The rabble from the bleachers swarmed the field. Warden Waller and the college president were on their feet, being congratulated by their subordinates as if they themselves had played the game. One of the umpires had secured the bat, another the ball (each designated a potential weapon), and were walking, arms across each other's shoulders, toward the clubhouse.

Starbuck was not at the canteen, nor was he in the bleachers. Phillip searched among the mob on the field. The red and the gold T-shirts had pretty much drained themselves out of the crowd, leaving a residue of mostly white with an occasional blue or maroon or dark green. Phillip looked for Starbuck's red cap or the glint of a Pepsi can. He searched for the big shining forehead or the low-pulled cap, the ears Starbuck had never learned to wiggle. He saw everyone but Starbuck. He looked again toward the bleachers, then the clubhouse, then the canteen. Nowhere was he to be found. The folding chairs were being folded, the top planks lifted down from the bleachers. Then he found him. He was shaking the hand of the college president.

From behind Phillip there was a sound like thick glass cracking in the cold. Another crack, then another. He and the librarian raced to the windows overlooking the parking lot. There on the ground were two of the college players, blood already spreading its dark stain outward on the dull gold T-shirts. One player was on his stomach, his right arm reaching out ahead of him on the pavement. The other was on his side, one leg bent back under him. Phillip continued to look. It was Butte, it was Folger. They had appropriated the opposing T-shirts and were now staining them with their blood, like ketchup making a sneaky triumph over mustard. Butte seemed to move the fingers of his right hand. Folger was completely still.

The blue Honda Phillip had seen before, its back doors wide open, was pulling away from the sprawled bodies. More shots were heard. The Honda kept going, the doors flapping like the wings of a panicked bird, as if the car were trying to take flight. Another shot, and the car stopped. The doors flapped two more times, one slammed shut, the other hung halfway open. A siren began to sound, then another, wailing, wailing for the fallen, for the dead.

There had been emergency lockup the rest of the afternoon and all that night. McTygue answered no questions except to give the final score: Chevaren Medium Security: 6; Chevaren Community College: 4. Medium Security dead: 2; Community College dead: 0.

The lockup lasted until late afternoon the next day. Dinner in the chow hall would be as usual that evening, with extra rations. Philip had tried to pass the time, to focus his concentration on something—anything other than the idiotic escape attempt and it's sickening climax. He had taken down the violin. The Bach *G-Minor* would provide the needed rescue from all other thoughts. But it was no use. He didn't even make it to the second voice of the fugue when the violin was returned to the shelf. He would give it another try, another time.

What happened next Phillip could understand without too much trouble. His understanding referred back to the death of his older brother George, who had become a fighter pilot in World War II. Phillip had been sent for at school just after lunch and told to go home. The telegram had come. George had been shot down in the Pacific near Okinawa, the plane and the body lost with no search possible.

People came to visit. Supper was quiet, the food brought over from the Tysons next door, roast chicken since chicken wasn't rationed, and baked potatoes and some Jell-O salad from Maggie Stowe down the block. Jokes were made when his grandfather got the wishbone. Phillip's sister Agnes—now Sister Rachel—would be home the next day and would stay at St. Aloysius convent until after the Requiem Mass.

That night, in his room, the room he'd shared with George, Phillip stood, panicked, at the side of his bed. He ached with the wish that someone would be there, in the bed, when he'd slip under the covers. He wanted another body there, not his brother, but someone who would hold him, take him into his arms, and the two of them would make love to each other. It could be anyone; just someone who would wrestle with him in the throes of sex, each abandoning himself to the other, doing all that could possibly be done—whatever that might be. He'd had no experience, no true notion of what could happen, but he needed to find out, then, there, that night. It shamed him that these were his thoughts at a time like this, but he couldn't help it. He yearned, he ached, he moaned without sound. Then, silently, he slipped in between the cold sheets, almost unbelieving that his desire, so urgent, so overwhelming, hadn't been able to force into being someone who would be waiting for him, someone who would answer his cravings. But no one was there, no one to help him prove with insatiable fury that he was alive and his brother was dead, no one with whom to share the sad glory of his triumph: he had won and his brother had lost.

George had been his idol and his comfort. George could do anything. He could build a fence, fix the vacuum cleaner, make a car run, put an aerial on the roof so there wouldn't be so much static on the radio. He could turn back flips, and he was going to buy a motorcycle when the war was over. He was going to be an engineer, just as Phillip was going to be a concert violinist.

Phillip had wondered, all the time George was in the war, if his brother, when he came home, would return to his bed. They had slept together for almost a whole autumn and a winter too, right after their sister, Agnes, had gone away. Even though they hadn't shared the same bed for a long time before George went into the Air Corps, Phillip had it somewhere in his mind that when George came back, he would come to him again the way he had come to him the night after Agnes had left. This, he figured, would only be fair. When Agnes had gone, George had Phillip to be with. But when George had gone, Phillip had no one. It seemed that George, after his return, should make compensation by providing Phillip with the comforts he'd been denied after his brother's departure. George had created the lack; George should provide the restitution.

On the afternoon of their first night together in Phillip's bed—on the day they took Agnes to the convent far up the river—Phillip and George had had a fight, right here in front of the convent where they'd taken Agnes. The convent was a huge mansion, of stones and towers and turrets, and it looked like a castle. They—Phillip and George and his grandmother and his grandfather—had said goodbye to Agnes and had kissed her, and she'd run across the grass and gone inside a big wooden door with panes of frosted glass.

They were walking back to the car his grandfather had borrowed from the Coogans so they could bring Agnes there themselves. They were on the grass, under some tall elm trees. The branches were waving and, since it was early September and the leaves had begun to dry, there was the lightest rustle as if mice were scurrying in the upper branches. George noticed he was still carrying the brown paper bag with the rest of the cookies in it, the ones their grandmother had baked for the trip— oatmeal with raisins. Agnes was supposed to have taken the rest with her. George stopped. "The cookies," he said. "Aggie forgot."

Phillip and his grandparents stopped too. They looked at the bag. It was grease-stained on one side and the top was twisted together like a rope where George was holding it. George looked back in the direction of the mansion. "She was supposed to take them with her." He took a step toward the mansion, way on the far end of a sloping lawn, then stopped. He brought the stained bag up to his face, his knuckles pressed against his nose. He began to cry. His shoulders heaved up and down, and he made singing sounds through his nose.

When he didn't stop, Phillip hit him in the stomach. He didn't say anything, he just hit him. After he'd hit him again and then a third time, grunting louder each time, George hit him back, on the cheek, with the paper bag. Phillip aimed upward for his face, but struck his chest instead. He was that much taller. George punched his shoulder, still making funny noises in his nose. Phillip began flailing at him with both hands, at his chest, his chin, his shoulders. George was now whacking the paper bag against Phillip's head. Phillip could hear the sudden roar of the paper brushing against his ear. He could hear the cookies disintegrating inside.

Their grandfather separated them. Their grandmother was appalled and said so. It was the first time Phillip had ever heard the word. On the ride back Phillip said nothing, looking out the window on his side. George, on his side, did the same.

That night, after George had come up to their room and gotten into bed—an hour after Phillip, because George was older—George, after a few minutes, got up out of his bed and climbed in with Phillip. Without either of them saying anything, they folded each other in their arms and stayed that way until Phillip—or maybe George—had fallen asleep.

For the next few months, George would spend about three minutes in his own bed, then come into Phillip's and hold him. Every night they slept that way, with no words said, no reference to it ever made. But it didn't last indefinitely. By spring, George was spending the whole night in his own bed. What Phillip missed was not only his brother's touch but his smell, a smell like warm beef stew. It was pungent and rich and Phillip had felt comforted, even protected by his brother's spiced and seasoned body. But then George was gone from his bed and Phillip could detect only faintly across the room the beef and onion scent that told him that his brother was still there.

On the night of his brother's dying, the cold air in the room was clear of all scents and smells, as clean as a winter night in an open field. He smothered his face in his pillow, struggling to catch the smell of someone other than himself, but there was only the scent of his oiled hair from the nights before and the lingering imprint of his own fevered flesh. He spread his arms out beyond the width of his bed and let the groans begin.

Phillip was tying his shoe when Starbuck came in. Starbuck stopped just inside the door, his hands behind him. "They got themselves killed," he said quietly.

"I know."

"They tried to escape. But they got themselves shot."

"Yeah."

Starbuck was looking down at the floor. "Can I sit next to you?"

"I'm not sitting. I'm standing."

"I mean, can you sit down? On the bunk? And can I come sit next to you?"

Phillip hesitated, as if his shoes were stuck to the floor, then he went to the bunk and sat down. He raised his left foot to check the shoelace, then pulled the knot tighter. Starbuck came to the bunk and sat down next to him. He kept looking down. "Can you put your arm around me? You don't have to if you don't want to. But could you anyway?"

Phillip put his arm across Starbuck's shoulders. The young man

109

simply nodded his head. "Do I still get to sit next to you when we go eat?" he asked. "I mean, they're dead now. You don't have to say we're hooked up anymore."

"Would you rather sit next to someone else?"

"Why would I want to do that?"

"For a change."

"Oh. That."

"Do whatever you want to do."

"Okay." He wiped his nose with the back of his hand. "I'll sit next to you. Even if they're dead." He reached his arm over and put it across Phillip's back. Neither of them moved. "Make love to me," Starbuck said quietly. "Please make love to me."

"You're scared is all. You'll be all right."

"I won't be all right. Please. You can pretend it's someone else. But please. I've got to do it with someone."

A door slammed somewhere down the tier. The grind of the grill gate was heard, then a loud click. Outside, far off, a freight train began its long rumble at the bottom of the gully, a defect in the track causing a clack, clack, clack at regular intervals like the strokes of an inexorable clock. Someone at the end of the tier called a name Phillip couldn't understand.

Starbuck raised his head, stared at the wall opposite, then looked down again. "Please?" He paused, then said, "I test negative and so do you. I gave Tummley in medical five dollars two weeks ago and he told me. We're both okay."

"Don't talk."

"You believe me, don't you?"

"Yes. I believe you."

"Then hold me. Please. Make love to me."

"Ssssh. Don't talk."

And so, very much to Philip's surprise, he and Starbuck had become lovers. Or perhaps it wasn't so much of a surprise after all. He had been first Starbuck's protector, and then, at the deaths of Butte and Folger, his comforter. Also, as if in preparation, he had awakened his body and prepared his flesh by the exercises, the naked, nighttime rituals he'd performed so he'd be ready to crack skulls when the proper time arrived. What was happening now seemed completely natural, a progression of events following an almost obvious course.

Then, too, Starbuck's nose stopped running. It was as though this effluvia had been a misguided mating signal, which, once answered, had become unnecessary. What pleased Phillip most, along with the exchange of simple human tenderness, was a newfound delight in what could only be called the life of negotiation, the necessary give and take of a shared existence where subtle compromises are effected without knowing they're compromises, where accommodation is made with lesser or greater awareness. He had forgotten the satisfactions that can come from unarticulated bargaining, the sense of achievement in making so complex an arrangement—two people as one—actually work.

It was as if Phillip and Starbuck, with their give and take, were weaving a many-colored cloth of uncertain pattern, its hues both blatant and somber, with threads of varying strength. Sometimes the weave would be close, sometimes loose. Only time would reveal the emerging pattern itself, its shifts, its struggles to shape itself. And time, too, would show it to be, quite possibly, a thing of great beauty, of fantastical design and sturdy knit, worthy to be shown to all the world, proclaiming the fidelity of both Phillip Manrahan and Talford Starbuck to the life of negotiation to which they'd committed themselves the day that death had come to dwell among them. It was from this cloth that Phillip would be willing to cut and stitch the robe that he must wear on the judgment day.

One other transformation took place. The huge scar on Starbuck's side failed to repel. When Starbuck had taken off his shirt that first afternoon, he had paused to let Phillip look at the distressed skin along his left ribs. The flesh was rippled and raw-looking, as if it had been chewed by some tiny teeth unable to take a good clean bite. It began about the middle of his rib cage and stopped just below his waist. It was the color of blood diluted with saliva; streaks of white, like unfinished skin, crossed and recrossed between the darker ridges. It seemed angry with itself, snarling and defiant.

Phillip had looked at the scar, saying nothing.

"You can change your mind if you want to." Starbuck waited, then began to put his T-shirt back on.

"No," Phillip said. "It doesn't make any difference. I haven't changed my mind."

The end, when it came, came quickly. In Phillip's unit they were getting undressed, Starbuck always slower than Phillip so that he could ask, "You want to take off my shorts for me?" Phillip would oblige and the gesture would lead them into their lovemaking. Tonight, just as Phillip had tugged the shorts down around Starbuck's ankles, he saw McTygue looking through the glass in the upper part of the door. Phillip kept right on doing what be was doing. He hoped to keep Starbuck from seeing the guard. He was afraid the young man would be frightened. They were, after all, subject for their infraction to a lock-in that could last three months.

Twice before Phillip had seen McTygue there at the door, but only after the lovemaking was in progress. It had been Phillip's impulse to jump up, open the door, drag McTygue into the room and, as brutally as possible, give him the sexual experience itself instead of allowing him to watch obscenely from the far side of the double glass. Phillip would have a quick vision of McTygue: terrified, protesting, promising, then stiffening into the pain until, at the end, he would be tossed back out the door, whimpering, disgraced.

It was at these moments that Phillip had finally known he was a prisoner, in a prison. Discipline, regimentation hadn't bothered him all that much; he could ignore lockups and head-counts; he could dismiss implicit scorn and overt contempt. But McTygue's power to insinuate himself into these moments with Starbuck was intolerable. This was the oppression the state had hoped to impose; this was the helplessness that was the true punishment for his crime; this was the exercise of the full power of the state against him that had been intended from the first. He must accept. He must not rebel; he must know that no revenge, no protest, was possible.

Both times McTygue had appeared, Phillip, in his rage, had simply continued his activities, maneuvering Starbuck into positions where he couldn't see the door. It was Starbuck who, all unknowing, would finally tame Phillip's wrath. So tender was this man that he could calm, with his lovemaking, all the savagery McTygue could arouse. So ardent was he that he could distract from even this most vile intrusion. And so sweet was he that he could, within moments, make Phillip feel newly blessed to hold him fast within his arms.

If Phillip felt any guilt at all it was because he had once scorned this very same man. He had found him inferior; he had believed him deserving of ridicule; he had dismissed him as an absurdity. But before Phillip could be overcome by shame, he would find forgiveness in Starbuck's touch, and on Starbuck's tongue, and know himself to be made worthy again and again of this dear good man's unending love.

Starbuck had lifted one leg and Phillip was pulling the shorts free, with the other leg still to go, when a key was turned in the lock. Starbuck jerked his head toward the door.

"Lift your foot," Phillip said.

Starbuck obeyed. McTygue stepped into the unit, closed the door and quietly stood there. Phillip, naked, stood up. Without looking at McTygue, he brought Starbuck close, gently placing his hand on the back of his head.

"McTygue's here," Starbuck whimpered.

"Yeah. I know."

"No, please—" McTygue said, "I don't really mean to interrupt. Just there's something I ought to tell you guys."

Phillip continued holding Starbuck close, a covering for his nakedness. McTygue tilted his head to the right. "Look, I'm not against you guys. Do I ever complain? But one thing I got to say. You guys, you're amazing, truly amazing, and I think I ought to let you know it."

Starbuck began to pull his head away from Phillip's shoulder, but Phillip increased the pressure of his hand and held it there. He looked at McTygue. The guard was about thirty-two, skinny, his dark brown hair neatly parted on the left and slicked back. He looked like he'd just been washed and combed for supper. The blue shirt of his uniform was tailored tightly around his upper torso. Apparently he liked being skinny and wanted everyone to see how little flesh he had on his bones. He leaned back against the door and crossed one ankle over the other. In his hand he held an unwrapped Snickers candy bar. "What amazes me most, Manrahan, is how it doesn't seem to bother you being so close to Starry like you are. Some guys couldn't do it. Look at him. You can see what he looks like. But you don't seem to care. Amazing. Not everybody could do that."

Phillip started to say something, but decided he'd just keep quiet. "You, Daddy," McTygue continued, looking closely at the Snickers bar, "you do all right though, for an old guy, don't you. Of course, I can see why. You're still in pretty good shape for someone your age. No sagging, except for that thing you're carrying around between your legs." He began tugging the paper on the Snickers, peeling it back as if it were a banana. Starbuck moved his head so that one ear was now pressed against Phillip's shoulder. Phillip relaxed his hold but still kept his fingers in among the wispy blond hair.

"But that dick you got, Starry, that wouldn't even make it past an asshole, that itty-bitty dick God gave you. Or is it just a pimple and I didn't look close enough?"

"It gets bigger," Starbuck whispered.

"Don't say anything," Phillip said. He put his nose down onto Starbuck's head and moved it lightly along the hair, making scratchy noises.

"And those feet of yours, Starry. Ever wash 'em, all cheesy like that?"

"I put aftershave on. They're all right now."

"Sssh." Phillip put his lips against the hair. It, too, smelled like aftershave. "Just let him talk."

"And you, Daddy, the way you don't care one little bit about all that pukey mess there on Starry's side. It really gets to me the way you can do what you do and pay it no attention at all."

Starbuck pulled away from Phillip as if to provide a better view of what McTygue was referring to.

"It doesn't bother you," McTygue asked, "I mean, to touch it and look at it or anything?"

"Why would it bother me? There's nothing wrong with it."

Starbuck, his head lowered, said quietly, "It was an accident. My old man, he didn't mean to do it. Why would he want to? I mean, hit me with scalding soup? I already told him I took the dollar. That's all he wanted, was to know did I take it. It was an accident." He took the undershorts from Phillip and held them against his side to shield the scar from McTygue's eyes.

"It looks like something you can lick off," McTygue said. "Like it's all sticky and maybe it's got sugar in it, and strawberries too. But don't worry. I'm not going to ask can I lick it. But it's so pretty there. Maybe I could just—you know, touch it. Is it okay if I touch it?"

Starbuck made no move. Phillip took one step toward McTygue. "I'm not going to hurt anything," McTygue said. "All I want is to touch it. You don't mind, Starry, do you? I do you some favors, now you do me a favor. Like let me touch it. So I know what it's made out of. If it's all sticky like it looks." Before any other movement could be made, McTygue put the tips of his fingers on the scar. "Uuuh. Feels even worse than it looks. Like scrambled egg only made out of wiggly stuff and blood." He uncurled his hand and let the open palm rest against the mottled skin. "Yeah. Now I can feel what it's like. How can anyone touch it? How can anyone even look at it?"

Starbuck raised his head and looked directly at Phillip. Neither of them moved. Slowly, slowly, McTygue rubbed the palm of his hand over the scar, up and down, then in slow circles. Helpless against it, Starbuck got an erection. He turned away, ashamed, angry. McTygue took in a deep breath, raised his shoulders, and closed his eyes. He let the breath out through his nose. Slowly he lowered his shoulders and opened his eyes. He let the tips of his fingers linger in among the ripples of flesh, then drew his hand away. He stepped back and shifted the Snickers bar into the hand that had been touching the scar.

"I think you want to go now, Mr. McTygue," Phillip said.

With his index finger, McTygue flipped Starbuck's penis. "I thought you said it got bigger." He went out, closing the door quietly behind him.

Starbuck began putting on his shorts, hopping on one foot, then the other. To steady him, Phillip reached out and took hold of his arm. "No!" Starbuck screamed. "Get away! You and everybody else. I don't want to be with anyone, ever. Finished. Finished, all of it!"

Phillip reached again, but Starbuck pulled farther away. "I know what I am. I know what I look like. I always knew, but for everybody's sake, I pretended I didn't. Even for you, for your sake, I pretended I didn't know I look funny. I even made believe I didn't have my scar, that I'm not all messed up like this. Even when I was with Evan and he was sick and I was taking care of him, I would pretend to myself I didn't have the scar, that Evan had someone good-looking to take care of him." He was hopping on one foot, holding the undershorts out in front of him, chasing them along the floor. "I was nice to him. I would tell him things that were funny and he'd laugh. That's why he told me the TV was mine, that he wanted me to have it after he died. Because I stayed there with him and cleaned him up and cooked him something he could try to eat. I could do all that because I was pretending it wasn't really me, that it was somebody good-looking, and didn't have a scar. It wasn't easy, doing it, but I did it. Pretended. All my life I've done it. But not anymore. I know what I am and what I look like. And I swear to God I don't care. I'm going to kill him. McTygue, I'm going to kill him. You wait and see. I'll get me a knife, and I'll stick him when he doesn't know, stick him right where he'll die, before he knows what's happened. You think I won't do it? You'll see!"

He stumbled against the toilet but kept his balance by stomping hard on the floor, one foot on the undershorts, as if he'd finally captured them. Without standing up straight, he said, "The TV was mine! Evan gave it to me. I had a right to go get it when his brother came and said everything was his. I had a right to go in, even if it was through the bathroom window. No one believes me that I had a right, and I don't care anymore." He stood up, holding the shorts with both hands, no longer trying to put them on. "I'm going to kill him. You'll see. And don't go expecting me to be nice and decent anymore and making people laugh like it's my job to do it. Not anymore, it isn't. The TV was mine! Evan gave it to me. It's mine, and I'm going to kill him!" He brought the shorts up to his face, sobbing into them.

In one swift movement, Phillip went down on his knees, reached his arms around Starbuck, and pressed his lips into the scarred side. Starbuck screamed as if the scalding soup had been thrown again. When Phillip held him even tighter, pressing his face deeper into the rippled flesh, Starbuck screamed again. "No! Don't!" He pulled away, terrified. With one hand, he made a fist. "Don't come near me. Don't touch me. Don't look at me. Don't!" He stretched his head back and let out a cry from somewhere deep in his chest.

Phillip stood up. He looked at Starbuck, then went to the door and looked out through the glass. McTygue was standing halfway down the corridor, leaning against the wall. He was examining the peeled Snickers again. He took a bite, then looked to see what effect the bite had had. He was licking his lips, bringing the candy bar closer to his face, ready for another bite.

Phillip reached up to the shelf and took down the violin. "Please don't play that thing," Starbuck said. "I can't stand it." Phillip braced the violin against his lower chest and turned the peg of the G-string toward himself. When the string came free, he followed its line down to the tuner and, loosening the loop that fastened it there, freed the string completely. Still naked, without looking at Starbuck, he went out the door.

McTygue, licking the back of the hand that held the Snickers, saw Phillip coming down the corridor. He took another bite, then looked again to see the pattern his teeth had made. When Phillip got to within a few feet of him, McTygue scrutinized the Snickers, then said, "You got a problem, Daddy?" Holding the candy bar away from him as if it were an ice cream cone and might drip on him, McTygue turned and started toward his desk, past the grilled gate.

Phillip came up behind him and caught the violin string under his chin, just above his Adam's apple. McTygue grunted and reached up, trying to tug the string away. Phillip, the coarse-threaded ends of the string wound tightly around his knuckles, pulled tighter. Then tighter still. A gagged cry came from McTygue's throat. Phillip jerked the neck, the head, closer to himself. Still clutching the candy bar, McTygue reached upward, trying to get at Phillip's eyes. He smeared chocolate onto Phillip's cheek, onto his chin, his neck, before he let the Snickers drop.

"Stop, Daddy! Don't!" Starbuck was at Phillip's arm, tugging then pummeling his back. "Don't, Daddy!"

Phillip kept his hold. McTygue moved his feet forward, his hands no longer able to reach upward. Phillip followed the way the feet led. McTygue began to slip slowly to the floor, his legs still struggling to run away. Phillip, making sure he hadn't slackened his grip, let the feet go where they wanted. By now McTygue's head was down to Phillip's waist and it looked, with McTygue's feet making quick little motions in one direction, then another, that the two men were playing "wheelbarrow," Phillip pushing, McTygue the wheelbarrow. Then the feet buckled under and McTygue was on his knees, his head falling forward.

"I won't kill him. I promise! Please, Daddy!" Starbuck's blows against Phillip's back, against his head, weakened, but he had begun to kick, first Phillip's calves, then his ankles. Phillip, from Starbuck's cries and blows, from McTygue's struggles, took new strength. He was getting stronger and stronger. Now it was he, Phillip, who was making the strangled sounds in the throat, now it was he who was gagging. His mouth open, his tongue pulled back behind his lower teeth, he pulled McTygue up, then held him against himself, his mouth at McTygue's ear. "No problem," he whispered. "No problem at all." He held his breath, then, with a long sigh, let one end of the violin string slip through his right fist. It slid quickly along McTygue's throat with the sound of a knife slit. The man slumped forward, his head falling near the remains of the candy bar, his eyes open, staring at the Snickers, his tongue sticking out toward it as if for one last lick.

Phillip took two deep breaths, then wound the violin string around his hand. Without looking down at McTygue, he strode back to his unit. Dawson and Bowersox had come into the corridor, but couldn't decide who to look at first, Phillip or McTygue, or at Starbuck who was poking the crumpled body and whimpering with each poke, "Mr. McTygue? He didn't mean it. Really, he didn't mean it. Mr. McTygue?" Only now did Phillip hear the bells going off, the shrilling for the express purpose of waking McTygue from his slumbers.

When they came to get him, rifles and pistols at the ready, Phillip, still naked, was sitting on his bunk. With one guard holding a pistol against his right temple and the muzzle of a shotgun against his left, he managed to rethread the G-string onto the violin before he was yanked up by no fewer than six hands. He was able to drop the violin safely onto the bunk before his arms were locked behind him and his head yanked backward by the hair. The movement brought to his nostrils the sickly swell of the smeared chocolate on his chin and on his cheek. It almost made him throw up, but he didn't want to disgrace himself in front of these gentlemen.

Now that Phillip had settled into his new cell—"settling in" consisting of sitting down on his bunk—he couldn't decide what to do first. Scanning the white, white walls, he tried to see if he could detect within its glossy surface the other colors of the spectrum that would have to be present to make the white white. No. He'd do that another time, working slowly, patiently, until he'd found everything from ultraviolet to infrared. He thought about Byronic times when, given nothing but a dank dungeon, he could have occupied his hours by making friends with the spiders and training the rats to jump and sit and beg and roll over and shake hands. If he had his violin he could play it, but because it was the murder weapon, it had been denied him. He'd been offered its carcass, unstrung, the offending gut removed, but he had politely declined.

Phillip surveyed the shining white space, then glanced up at the caged light bulb on the ceiling. He had been given at last the answer to a modern mystery. Inside the refrigerator, when the door is shut, the light does stay on.

SEVEN

The stairs were not the problem Rachel had expected them to be. Mother came down sideways, both hands clutching the banister, bringing one foot, then the other, down onto each step before attempting the one below. Mother had told Rachel to walk in front of her. If she fell, Rachel would break the fall, and they could both tumble together with less damage to Mother than to Rachel. Slowly Rachel went down, making sure she wasn't too far ahead, walking erect as if she were making some ceremonial entrance down the grand staircase. With Mother bent, almost crouched, behind her, it seemed, however, that Rachel was hiding the old woman, unwilling to let anyone know that she was there.

Mother was to be shown the painting of *The Last Supper* on the refectory wall. It was finished. Worried that she might have been rushing the job, Rachel had purposely slowed herself, easing the brush strokes, reworking a hand, a fold of clothing, enriching a color she had once considered sufficient, deepening flesh tones to make sure the faces had a full and vibrant life. She'd had to assure herself that she wasn't rushing Mother's death. Mother, after all, had promised to live to see the finished painting. Once she'd seen it, she could go ahead and die. Rachel did not want Mother to die; still she had to admit that she wanted to be free so she could go see her brother. But she would not consider herself free until after Mother's death. It was she, Rachel, to whose care Mother had been given. She could not desert the dying woman in her final hours.

But of course, she could—and easily. All she had to do was ask Sister Martha or Sister Cathrael to take over for the two days it would take her to get to the prison and come back. There was no question that they might refuse. Sister Martha's hungry and homeless would be fed in her absence; a volunteer could surely be found in an emergency. Sister Cathrael's work in the Chancery, overseeing the dissolution of the Order, meeting with clergymen and with lawyers, could easily be postponed. If the Order were to survive one or two days more, it would hardly be considered a calamity. An inconvenience to the bishop, perhaps, but hardly a calamity.

The truth was that Rachel was unwilling to surrender Mother's death to anyone but herself. Her love for the Mother General was beyond dispute; she had considered it an honor to be allowed to care for her. But like most honors, it had prompted pride. And jealousy. She must preside over Mother's death. She, and she alone, must witness the last breath. She must close the revered eyes and place the first kiss of farewell on the forehead of the stilled body. No one but she. For this reason, Rachel had not gone to see her brother. She was afraid Mother might die while she was away, that all her patient labors would be without their ultimate reward, that the honor promised her would be appropriated by another.

So she would remain at the bedside, sleeping on a quilt on the floor, alert to every sound, every shift in the bed, every moan, every breath. She would dispense the medicines, bring the food, bring the lightly sipped drink. She would sit patiently in the chair, accepting finally the dictum of speaking only when spoken to. She would cool the fevered face and wash the fouled body. She would lightly hold the fragile hand or touch the waxen cheek so that Mother would know, in her flesh, that she was not alone, that she was loved, that someone blessed her, even if the benedictions came from a hand that would soon steal away to work on a painting downstairs.

To navigate their way across the great hall, they locked arms and moved very cautiously, almost stealthily, over the vast expanse of linoleum beneath their feet. On the far side, they reached the refectory door, the door to what had been the main dining room in the baronial days of the mansion's past. Rachel sat Mother in a chair, then pulled out a key from her smock pocket and unlocked the door with a swift click like the single chirp of a self-assured robin. The door was rolled open like a barn door, sliding back with a rumble and a few bangs into its slot. Rachel then squatted down in front of Mother and had her circle her arms loosely around her neck. With her hands at Mother's waist, Rachel lifted her up, easily, steadily suppressing the urge to say "Whee."

"The best way to see it," Rachel said, leading Mother through the door, "is to walk to the windows, then turn around and look."

"It smells so fresh in here," Mother said. "Paint always smells so fresh. And turpentine too. Here's where I should have come for a breath of fresh air." They stopped while Mother took in a long satisfied breath. "Ah, fresh paint. Lovely, lovely." Together they headed for the windows on the far side of the room.

"Look," Mother said. "The vines on the carriage house, the leaves are turning. Isn't it early for that?"

"It's October, Mother."

"Ah, yes, October."

When they reached the four high windows that looked out onto the back grounds, Mother stood there, moving her head from side to side. "October," she said.

The grass was patterned with leaves, yellow, red, and brown, but mostly yellow from the locust trees. Gently they lay, like manna rained down from above that no one wanted anymore. A squirrel was offering its reflection to the birdbath, jerking its head from side to side, checking this profile, then that. The brick carriage house at the far end of the rose garden was covered completely with reddened vine leaves like arrested fire, flickering only when a chance wind moved among them. The sky was a lighter gray than the slate roof of the carriage house, and more evenly colored. Against it, the weather vane, a replica of the shoe in which the old woman lived who had so many children she didn't know what to do—a piece of whimsy indulged in by the original owner who had no children—pointed its toe to the northeast. Above and beyond was the line of pines that gave the mansion its western border.

"October," Mother repeated. Slowly she shook her head, whether in disbelief or awe, Rachel couldn't tell. She kept a firm hold on Mother's elbow, looking mostly at the weather vane, wishing it would move, that it would twirl in the wind and give them both a sudden delight. "Sit here," Rachel said, pulling a chair closer with her foot. "Then you can see. But wait until I turn on the lights. Close your eyes, and I'll tell you when you can open them."

Mother let herself be helped into the chair, not knowing at first what to do with her hands. The chair had no arms. She put her hands on her lap, then gripped the side of the chair itself to hold herself as erect as possible. Rachel turned on the chandelier, then the wall sconces. "You can look now," she said.

Mother opened her eyes. Her head didn't move, nor did any muscle on her face. She seemed not even to blink. Rachel said nothing. She came quietly back to Mother's side and stood slightly behind her. She, too, looked at the painting. It covered the entire wall, its bright and glaring colors, each fierce in its own insistence, each raucously knocking against another. To keep them separated, she'd outlined the shapes in black, then reverted to the old admonition to color inside the line. She hoped the painting wasn't too cluttered. There had been so much she'd wanted to include. Her greatest discontent was with the lettering above the painting and below. She had tried for a script copied from the Psalter and might have obscured some of the letters, an *I* looking like a *T*, an *S* looking more like a seahorse than a letter of the alphabet. "This is my body," it said above; "This is my blood," it said below.

Mother was pushing against the seat of her chair, struggling to stand. Rachel touched her shoulder, an attempt to persuade her not to get up. "Take your hand away," Mother said.

"But—"

"Take it away."

Rachel obeyed, but only halfway, ready to reach again if necessary. Mother got to her feet and steadied herself with one hand on the back of the chair. She did not take her eyes from the painting. She reached toward the far wall and made a forward lunge. Again she steadied herself, her hand now on the edge of the massive refectory table. Rachel made a move closer, but Mother reached her other hand behind her and flapped it several times, warning her off. Hand over hand along the table's edge, she made her way toward the painting. At the end of the table, the one close to the pantry door, she stopped, still not taking her eyes from the figures on the wall before her.

"Do you remember their names?" Mother asked.

"I—I'm not sure. I think so. Yes."

"Tell me. Tell me their names."

Rachel, for her *Last Supper*, had painted not the Holy Apostles and Our Lord at their Passover meal, but the sixth grade in the lunchroom, on the noonday of the fire that would kill them all. There they were, five at each table, the tables themselves made of white oak, with ladder-back chairs to match. Most of the children could touch the floor with their feet but a few let their legs dangle, with two of the girls hooking their shoes into the rungs beneath the seats. It had been early spring, April, after Easter, with everyone still wearing a sweater, V-necks for most of the boys, cardigans for the girls. Green had been the favorite color that year, with blue a fairly close second, then maroon, two yellows, one red, and one black. Some of the girls wore plaid pleated skirts with white blouses, red plaid, navy plaid; others had on dresses, starched cotton, pastels mostly, with wide collars and fronts decorated with pearl buttons or white piping. The boys wore long woolen pants, gray, dark blue, black, with only one pair of brown. Those who weren't wearing a tie had their shirts buttoned at the neck. The girls' hair was long, the boys' short, and everyone was neatly combed. More than several of the girls wore barrettes and one had a white satin ribbon pulling her hair back from her ears. One boy wore a wristwatch; three girls had rings.

The lunchroom tables were a clutter of brown paper bags and waxed paper; apples, oranges and bananas, half-sandwiches in some places, cookies, waited on the waxed paper. It was early in the lunch period; everyone was still eating the first half of the first sandwich. Most had their elbows on the table, but a few were sitting back, a half-sandwich resting on a lap or being raised to an open mouth. Two girls and a boy had one elbow on the table so they wouldn't seem too obedient. Each had a half-pint bottle of milk and a sipping straw.

Sister Louise, her black garb and white wimple in contrast to all the color around her, was listening with wide-eyed delight to the girl with the hair ribbon. In front of her, ignored, were some papers she'd brought along to correct while monitoring the lunchroom. She seemed to be the only one not talking. Everyone, without exception, had been given beautifully shaped lips, very red, just as they had been given clear and beautiful eyes. Most were facing front, but those in profile, to make up for the loss of an unseen eye or only half a mouth, were given larger noses.

Along the top edge of the painting, on the line beneath the ceiling, was what seemed at first an attempt at a frame, a scalloped decoration of loops, red with streaks of black. Then they were recognized not as decoration but as small tongues of fire, not yet descended.

Mother made her way around the refectory table. She reached out a hand and lurched toward the right side of the painting where a girl in a blue dress and yellow sweater was sipping her milk. Mother's open hand braced itself against the painting, stopping a fall. Without taking the hand from the wall, she slid it up and touched the ear of the boy with the wristwatch.

"The names," she said. "What was his name?"

"Joey Calto," Rachel said quietly. "He drew pictures better than anyone in the whole sixth grade."

Mother moved her hand to the left, raising it higher, to the hair of a girl in a light green dress and blue sweater. "Susan Darnell," Rachel said. "She had five brothers, all older." Quickly, Mother slid her hand to the head of a boy wearing an orange and green tie. "Billy Cometti. He had the most beautiful brown eyes I'd ever seen."

As Mother moved her hand across the painting and down, then up again—lightly touching the faces with only the tips of her fingers, the hair, the bright clothing—Rachel spoke their names. "Jonathan Ross. He had to fight a lot because his father was a garbage man. Debbie Hall. She was going to be an airline stewardess, she said. Roland Peck, Tom Goodrich, Roger Eveleth, he had such beautiful penmanship, Connie Fitzgerald, Joseph Anclien, Steven Fanto, Miriam Lee, Randy Fong. . . ."

Rachel spoke the names simply, her voice even and low. Mother was reaching up now, toward a boy in a maroon sweater and a white shirt buttoned at the neck. He was holding part of his sandwich against his cheek and reaching over to touch the shoulder of the girl next to him. Rachel said the name, "Tony—" The last name was swallowed. She didn't move, nor did Mother, Mother's fingertips still touching the cheek of the boy. Slowly she brought the hand down, moving it through the painting, through the hair, the mouths, the sandwiches, the cheeks and eyes of the feasting children. Her body, at the same time, lowered itself until she was crouched down near the floor. Rachel went to the end of the table and waited. Mother, her right hand still raised up into the painting, resting on the lips of the girl with the pearl buttons on her dress, put her forehead against the wall. Rachel moved closer.

"Oh God," Rachel heard Mother whisper. "Oh God, take from us our hearts of flesh and blood, and give us hearts of stone." Her arm dropped to her side, but she lifted it again to push herself away from the wall.

Rachel bent down and reached out a hand to touch her, but drew it back. After another moment, she whispered, "Mother?" Mother didn't move. Rachel touched her shoulder, letting her fingers rest there, then put her hand on Mother's head. The hair was as soft as smoke. "Mother?

Did you hear what I was saying? I knew their names. They'd all been taken from me, when I was cured. But they're back."

Mother reached out her hand and touched Rachel's cheek. "Yes. They're back. They're here." She let the hand fall away, onto the floor. "Now take me home," she said.

Gently Rachel helped her stand; gently she put her hand around Mother's waist, letting the old woman's head fall against her shoulder. She began to guide her toward the door, past the huge refectory chairs, the massive table. She was tempted to look back, to see again the returned children, but decided not to. She had painted the painting, and the painting had brought the children back to her. Mother now had seen it and heard her speak the names. It was finished, it was done. The great mansion would come down, the stones knocked one from the other, the wall pulverized, the bright flecks of paint, blue, green, red, yellow, glinting out through the dust.

As they crossed the great hall, Mother slumped against Rachel, unable to walk farther. Rachel, without asking, simply reached behind her, one arm across Mother's back, the other behind her shoulders, and lifted her up again.

So little did Mother weigh that Rachel moved too fast and Mother almost flew out and away from her arms. After gathering the birdlike body against her, she continued across the great hall and started up the stairs. Halfway to the landing, Mother said, "Here. We'll stop here." Rachel went up two more steps, but Mother repeated the words, "Here. We'll wait here. The two of us."

Rachel sat her down on the step and let her lean her head against a column of the banister. The head rolled slightly from side to side before settling into a groove of the spiraled balustrade. Mother whispered her thanks, slowly closing, then opening her eyes. On her lips was a sly and distant smile, as if she had not quite decided to tell Rachel something, something that would be beyond her understanding. Each breath was held as if caught by some question, then released after a decision had been made. The respirations became shallow, but they seemed to have gathered into themselves a deeper cough, an angry gargle like an impatient protest. Mother's waxen flesh was smooth, the tallow beneath the skin no longer golden but now a clouded gray, like smudged silver.

Mother was reaching her right hand out when another breath, long in coming, caught her body, bouncing it twice, harshly, brutally, against the balustrade. The fingers that had hoped to touch Rachel's cheek now clawed at it, scoring the flesh; then the hand fell down along Rachel's shoulder and across her breast before flopping itself onto her lap. To the colors on Rachel's smock was added a small spot of red no larger than a raindrop.

Rachel searched Mother's face, the half-lidded eyes, the slack mouth, the cheeks, the forehead, looking for the place from which the next breath might come. When the great heaving didn't repeat itself, when no breath came—no matter how hard Rachel might look—she shifted herself closer to Mother, the two or them sitting there, on the same step. Once more she searched the unmoving face, willing to accept an inhalation from anywhere. Perhaps the eye would take in the air. New ways could be found. Other means of life were surely there if only Rachel could find them, if only Mother would be willing to give them this final chance. The ear, the pores, each could become a mouth, breathing in the air, breathing it out. They must try. Mother must make them try.

But all attempts were withheld and no breath came. No final orders were issued, no directives sent forth. Rachel herself breathed slowly in and out three times, an example and a prod, an experiment in what it would be like to draw breath from an air unshared by the woman at her side. Her own breathing, she discovered, changed nothing; the air had not changed, nothing had changed except that Mother had died.

Rachel gathered her up again, careful that her head should fall comfortingly onto her chest. When she turned to start up the stairs, her right foot stumbled on the step below, and she had to bring her knee up quickly to support the body in her arms. After she'd steadied herself, she pressed her foot firmly onto the step, forcing the wood beneath the linoleum to squeal, admitting its subjection to her foot.

As they mounted the stairs, great blares of gold, then red, then blue, then green hit against them from the window above, but they didn't stop. One after the other the colors came, blades of light, slashing through them, blue and green, shards of red, great strokes of gold, stabbing through their bodies, but still they continued, unflinching, unafraid of all that glory.

EIGHT

If the white, white cell had surprised Phillip, this visiting room
surprised him more. He had expected a dingy replica of the one room
at Chevaren, grimy floors spotted with spat-out gum, a table and wooden
chair, heavy to discourage their being thrown at someone, or worse, a
counter bisected by a screen of wire mesh separating the visitor from the
convict. But again his expectations had been faulty. The room was at least
four times the size of his cell, and if it wasn't exactly a comfortable living
room, it approached in size and decor the waiting room of a well-heeled
dentist, minus the magazines and the plants and the pictures of Mexico.

There were three cushioned chairs, comfortable, and covered with
real leather, not Naugahyde, two of them somewhere between tan and
orange, and the third a green darker than the tiles covering the floor.
(Real tiles, it seemed, not plastic.) The room was not glaringly lit as he'd
expected, but had track lighting along two sides of the high ceiling.
There were three windows, also high up, out of reach, one of them
open—in concession to penal attitudes—at a slant, with its top pulled
into the room, preventing any view of the sky.

His sister Aggie was coming to visit. He wanted to see her, to make sure she was all right—whatever *that* might mean. But he didn't want her to see him, not in his present "situation." But since his "situation" would change only when the switch was thrown, he knew he'd better do now what had to be done and make the best of it.

He would tell Aggie about the embezzled money. It would distract her from the murder. They could even laugh at last at what he'd done. She could pretend to be scandalized. He would tease her, telling her she was secretly pleased, secretly proud. But this came too close to the coy.

He could tell her about his love for Talford Starbuck, how he would give his life if he could be allowed—for just one single moment—to lie down again at his side. But what good would telling her do now? Besides, he'd already given his life; no appropriate extravagance was left to be offered, so he should just forget the whole thing, or at least not trouble his sister about it.

Maybe she could tell him about her own life. The Mother General, he'd been told, had died. The Order was being dispersed. She'd painted a painting. The old Motherhouse was being torn down. She was to go to the bishop's residence to scrub floors and polish furniture. But no, that hardly seemed appropriate for their final conversation.

He'd think of something else. Not the killing. Not the electrocution. And certainly not sin and salvation, repentance and redemption. He knew the words, but he also knew that they hardly applied to him. The faith to which he had been born—his sister's faith—had long since been taken from him and he had not the least inclination to ask that it be returned. So harshly had it been snatched away that he had even come to believe it had never existed to begin with.

What had occasioned his expulsion was, of course, his sexual proclivity—about which he could do nothing. He remembered very well the pastor of his parish telling him not to come to confession again until he'd freed himself of this unacceptable form of corruption. Phillip considered telling him, in all sincerity, that if he freed himself, there'd be no need to return, but *be* didn't think Father McPherson would understand. To Father McPherson, what he considered Manliness was next to Godliness, with Manliness slightly elevated above its beatific buddy.

Phillip had, in those days, prayed desperately that the changes demanded by Father McPherson be achieved, and with a little heavenly assistance. His prayer was answered but, as so often happens with prayers, the answer was no. Which seemed only fair considering the similar response given by the Almighty to generation upon generation of leopards who'd repeatedly begged that their spots be changed.

At sixteen, Phillip had tried to bargain with God. Granted a switch in instinct, he'd have twelve children, an overload of offspring being the proof of piety preferred by most clergy at the time. Again, the answer was no, probably to protect the poor unsuspecting female who might unwittingly have found herself a party to the bargain—the woman who would not only bear, deliver, and raise his twelve squalling bribes, but would have to sustain herself as well through Phillip's sweaty efforts to make good on his promise.

When he was eighteen and his sexual experiments had proved successful and become certified practice, Phillip was told to either revise (falsify) the data on which his findings were based and thereby reverse the conclusions of his findings, or leave the church. If he could not commit sins of a more acceptable sort or unsex himself completely—something of a vow of self-castration to which he knew he had not been truly called—he must stop frustrating confessors who knew of no other remedy than complete schism.

And so Phillip did as he was told: he left. On occasion, since then, rumors would reach him that he would soon be sent for, that the good news had already been spoken, that he would be told he must return. He could even hear, from time to time, the distant creak of the ancient gate, struggling to open, but then a gust of wind, usually issuing from the mouth of some scandalized hierarch who believed the Universal Church best fulfilled its universality by the unremitting exercise of its unbounded power to exclude, would slam it shut. Phillip would have to remind himself—again—that he must struggle as best he could without the patrimony of grace he'd been brought up to expect, that the great fund of blessings he'd been told were his legacy was fast secured by purse strings often interlaced among fingers bearing a cardinal's ring or even the Seal of Peter, and that there were no plans afoot to dole out any of its treasure to the likes of him.

The prison authorities, however, probably in response to some bureaucratic directive, had sent him a priest, Father Singh, a young man from India. (America, it seemed, had become again mission territory, recruiting its priests from foreign lands.) The session had been reasonably brief. Father Singh was a short man, his skin a uniformly pale brown with no heightening or deepening of color, which gave the impression of equanimity, even serenity. His eyes were large and round and almost black, like those of a boy still susceptible to amazement. He seemed inordinately skinny, like a planed board, but the cut of his black suit, trim but not tight, indicated no loss of weight. He would have been a perfect jockey. He was, in fact, perfectly proportioned, but in miniature, the features of his face, his hands, feet, ears, even his haircut all in an easy and amiable relation one to the other. Maybe the round eyes were too expectant, but that seemed a spiritual, not a physical property. His hair, as black as it could be without turning purple, seemed a crowning award, a mark of approval set on his head with great satisfaction by a justly pleased creator.

After Father Singh, sitting on the bunk without invitation, had asked Phillip if there was anything he could do for him and had been told no thank you, the priest apologized for coming without an invitation. Even though Phillip had insisted when he entered prison—both here and at Chevaren—that he was of no particular faith, it was noted that he had a sister who was a nun, which accounted for the present intrusion. After Phillip assured the priest that his sister's calling in no way affected his own spiritual or religious status, Father Singh slapped himself on the knees, got up from the bunk, and started toward the door.

"All right," he said. "If you say so. The one thing I never do is pressure anyone. I'm not here to make you feel agitated. I'll hear your confession, bring you the Eucharist, anytime you want me to. But I'm not going to pester you about it. For one thing, I don't have the time. Or, I have to admit, the energy. If anything's to be done, God will have to do it. Or you." He stopped at the door and shook his head. "I have too much to do as it is." He turned and held out his hand. "Well, Mr. Manrahan, this may be the last time we see each other, so maybe we should say goodbye. Huh?" He was smiling. Phillip searched the smile for mockery. He looked into the eyes for cunning. But he found neither. The young priest had meant what he'd said. They shook hands. Father Singh turned toward the door and rapped against the metal. Before the guard could begin clanking the bolts and letting loose the air pressure that would release the door, he said without turning back, "You may think I'm being clever, leaving you on your own like this, but I'm not clever at all. I'm simply very, very tired."

Now he did turn around, and the dark eyes had made themselves even darker by retreating farther back into the surrounding bones. "Goodbye, Phillip Manrahan. Goodbye." The guard's head in profile, snub nose and all, appeared behind the grillwork. The air was released; the door slid almost silently open, and Father Singh stepped quickly through.

Phillip got up from his chair in the visiting room. There was nothing he and his sister could talk about. There was nothing that could be said. She must not come to see him. He should go to his electrocution without involving her in any way. But just the thought of "electrocution"—in the context of a visit from his sister—took on a foolish and simple irony. His execution would have its similarities to his sister's treatments. Electric shock was obviously deemed efficacious for them both. Anguish beyond bearing had been his sister's crime, and she had been duly punished. Despair beyond acceptable limits had been her sin and the proper penance had been quickly imposed. Through her body the killing current ran— into her brain, piercing its way, pillaging, putting to the sword all that had offended. And she had offended mightily. That she herself had been suffering was bad enough, but it was Phillip's own pain at the sight of her, at the thought of her—his sister—savaged by grief, made insensible by loss—that had made him complicitous to the barbarity inflicted on her. It was his suffering, not hers, that he had wanted most to dispel. It was to end his own helplessness and anguish that he'd put his name to the hospital form. It was to free himself from pain that he'd agreed to the brutal prescription. For his sake, his sister had been divested of all that she had been, and relieved of all that had been promised her. Dignity and intellect had been torn away, joy and certitude had been forbidden to her from that time on. With those few pushes of a pen, the careful cursive that had always been his pride, Phillip had rejected his suffering. He would not bear it. If his sister must cease to be, then she must cease to be. He must go on, unimpeded by pain. And to that determination he had set his name in blackest ink, right on the dotted line.

But now he seemed to have found a way—through what subterranean maze he could not trace—to experience the same "process" he had helped to inflict on her. Although this offered him no real sense of expiation, he did appreciate the similarities. Aggie, without being aware of it—much less requiring it—was being given her revenge, and he would be the last to deny it to her now.

The door opened, and a tall woman with short unruly hair entered the visiting room. Phillip stopped his breath and held it halfway through an inhalation. He took a step backward, staring at the woman. She was beautiful. To steady himself he put the tips of his fingers on the arm of a chair. This was his sister, Aggie, and she was beautiful. The years had taken all the extraneous flesh from her face and had lined it along the sides of the nose and mouth with creases that made greater the dignity and strength inherent in all her features. Her eyes, a darker brown than he remembered, were softened by a puzzled resignation but made strong by a determination not to be weary. The chin was raised as if the curve of her neck was the one vanity she'd still allow herself.

"Aggie?" he whispered.

"Peppy?"

She was wearing a light blue skirt, a pink blouse with a tiny collar too dainty for her, and a brown woolen cardigan that seemed too thin for the chill in the room. There was on the skirt itself what looked like a maroon smudge of paint just above the knee. She took a step into the room. Her arms started to rise from her sides as if she were going to reach out and gather him in, but she lowered them abruptly, then pressed her hands against her skirt.

"I'm late," she said, looking down at her hands. "The man driving me here—I don't have a license—I mean, I haven't driven since—I haven't driven for so long, so a man was hired to bring me here and take me back. And I shouldn't have told him to go faster. He almost got a ticket, but when I said I was—Sister Rachel, on my way to visit here, the man, the driver, he only got a warning. But I'm late, and I'm sorry."

"Maybe they'll let you stay past the time." He could only whisper.

"No, it's all right. I didn't want to be here too long anyway. I mean—no, I didn't mean that. I want to be here. But it won't take me all that long to—to—"

When she didn't continue, Phillip said, but still very quietly, "Come. Sit down. Please."

She started toward the chair farthest away from him. His eyes followed her. He must be careful. He must do nothing that might distress her. She sat down, but didn't lean back into the chair. She seemed prepared to leave at any moment. Phillip sat in the dark green chair, not the one directly opposite her, but another one, angled a little to her right. She was looking at him now, and it seemed that her eyes were being attacked by something that made her wince repeatedly.

"Are you warm enough?" Phillip asked, still unable to raise his voice much above a whisper.

"They kept my coat." She tried to smile. "But I'm all right. I can button up my sweater if it gets cold." He nodded.

She folded her hands on her lap. "Do they treat you all right?"

"Oh yes."

"I was told I couldn't bring anything to eat. I thought maybe some cookies, but they said definitely no."

"I get plenty. Not cookies, but enough to eat, I mean."

"Good."

Aggie looked at her thumbs, crossed there on her lap. She raised one as if to make sure it could move, then lowered it. "Is it warm enough, where they have you?"

"Oh yes."

She nodded her head, then raised her thumb again, watching it carefully as she lowered it. "They told me I wouldn't be allowed to come to—" She stopped and sat up even straighter in the chair, "to the execution." She blinked once, then looked directly at him. "I asked again, but was told nothing could be done to change it." She blinked twice. "Was that your decision?"

"The warden. No immediate family." He looked down at the tiles on the floor. They were tightly placed. The lines could have been drawn with a pen. He looked more closely to make sure it wasn't just a grid design made to seem like individual squares. But they were squares, individually placed.

"I won't stay long," she was saying. "But there's one thing—just one really—that I came to tell you about. But first I—is it all right if I ask you something?"

"Why not? If you want to."

"I wouldn't bother you with it but I'm so—so confused."

"What is it?"

"I was told that at—at the trial—or the hearing or whatever it was— I was told that at first the lawyer they got for you, he said you—you did what you did to—keep someone else from doing it. From—you know—the guard. That you were afraid or you thought this someone else was going to—you thought someone else was going to do it, so you did it. To save him. That you didn't want to—to kill the man so much as you wanted to save someone who was going to do it. Is—is that true?"

Phillip looked down. When he spoke his voice was still quiet. "No. Not really."

"What do you mean, not really?"

"Maybe at first, yes, but then—when I'd started—" He paused, then asked, "Do you really want to hear this?"

"I think so. Please. Go on."

Phillip waited a moment, then said, "Maybe at first that was what I was thinking—that I was afraid Starbuck might do it, so I'd do it myself before be could. But when I'd started, when I felt him, the guard, McTygue— when I felt him struggling—I knew I was doing it for myself. He was grasping and fumbling and trying to get away with tiny little steps, but I wouldn't let him. He thought he could humiliate my—my lover, Starbuck—the man I loved—that he could make him despise himself. He wanted my—my lover to hate himself—and nothing would happen to him, to the guard, to McTygue. No. He couldn't do that and then nothing would happen. That's what I decided. When he began struggling is when I realized that. And that's when it turned out to be me who wanted to kill him. For myself. I wanted it to be me—and only me—who did it. I wanted to squeeze the begging right out of him. Who was humiliated now? Now who despised himself? Now who had the power and who was helpless! All I could do was pull tighter. Despise? Humiliate? Tighter— tight—! I'd finally become who I really am."

"No!" Rachel had jumped up and was starting toward the door. She stopped, waited a moment, then took another step away from Phillip. She reached out her hand, trying to touch the door. She was going to knock, to ask for release. She raised her hand and held it there. She stood for a moment, not moving, then turned and went slowly back toward the chair. Her head was bowed; her hands were at her sides. "No, I don't want to hear," she said quietly. "But yes, yes, I want to hear. You're my brother, Peppy, and I should know these things." She sat down, again without leaning back.

"I'm sorry," Phillip said. "I shouldn't have said anything." Rachel moved her head slightly but kept looking down at her hands. "Do you want to go now?" Phillip asked. "You can if you want to."

"Yes, I want to leave now. But I'm not going to. I don't want to be here. But I am."

"You said you had something you came to tell me."

"Yes."

"What is it?"

"It doesn't seem to matter now. Nothing does."

"Tell me anyway. Then it'll be time, and you can go." He waited, then added. "Tell me. Please."

Rachel looked down at her hands as if she had been holding crib notes but now couldn't find them. She moved her head first to one side, then the other, searching the floor around her chair. She looked again at her empty hands. "When I was told you did it to keep someone else from doing it, they said it was—the way you just said, that it was for a lover. The Starbuck you mentioned. At first I wasn't sure what that meant. I had to—to think about it. I had to think about—about the two of you. I know what it means now. I don't understand it. But I know it. I want to understand it—and I will. But not yet. Is—is that all right?"

"It's nothing you have to think about."

"But it is. It's you. I have to think about you. How can I think about you and not think about who you are?"

Phillip reached over and touched the arm of her chair. "You still haven't told me what you were going to tell me. Tell me now. Please. What is it?"

Rachel separated her hands and curled her fingers inward, rubbing them against the palms as if trying to restore circulation in the numbed flesh. When she'd folded her hands again, she said, "There were so many things I didn't want to say, so many things I didn't want to hear, I thought I would just tell you something—from a long time ago, then get up and leave. But now—"

"Please. Something from a long time ago. I want to hear it. There isn't anything else we need to say. Not really. Tell me, Aggie."

"I thought it would let you know, now, here, with what's happening—that it would let you know—let us both know that—"

"That what?"

"That you'd been happy. That we all had. But you especially. Really, truly happy."

"Then tell me. Please."

140

"You won't remember it because you were barely three." She began clenching her hands more firmly into each other. "I was ten," she said, "and George was eight, I guess. We were at the river, and Momma and Daddy were there and we were all swimming, down below Conlon's cove, having a picnic under the trees with potato salad and watermelon after, and baloney sandwiches with mustard on. And, oh, olives. The first time I ever had an olive and at first I didn't like them, but Momma kept saying *Ummmmm* when she was eating hers so I tried another one and Daddy kept spearing one out of the jar with his jackknife, and then another one and giving them to George, so I kept eating them too and by the time the jar was empty, I liked them. I still do. Green olives." She stopped and shook her head. "You had on your good rompers and under them a thin rubber pair of pants to keep you from wetting all over everyone. For you to go in swimming, Momma took off the rompers, and you'd have on just the pants. You had such a belly then, we all had to laugh, the way the elastic came down below this fat little tummy, and the way you kept showing us your belly button, you were so proud of it.

"At first you didn't want to go into the water, but Daddy put you on his shoulders and walked out, telling you how good it felt, until the water touched your little feet and then covered them up. Instead of putting you right into the river, Daddy walked back to where the willows were and set you down on the pebbles and took your hand and the two of you walked out into the water, him telling you again how good it felt, and Momma too, sitting under the tree eating watermelon and pinching the seeds like they were tiddlywinks so they'd shoot into the leaves hanging down from the willow. You walked until the water came up to your belly, and then you came back. But what Daddy did then is what I came to tell you. He sat down in the water, just at the edge of the river, and put you onto his right leg, your back up against his huge foot so you wouldn't fall over backward. He held onto both your hands with his, and then he dunked you up and down into the water so it came just up to your chest. He kept dunking you and yelling 'Whooops' and you would laugh! Oh, Peppy, you screamed and squealed and Momma too was saying 'Whoops,' and George out in the river kept calling you to swim out to him. Oh, Peppy, you were so *happy*. And Momma and Daddy and George—all of us—you especially—we were all so happy and Daddy kept dunking you down into the water and coming out again. You were sitting there on Daddy's leg, against his foot and the foot big enough so you wouldn't fall over backward."

She stopped and looked first to her right, then to her left as if confused.

"What happened then?" Phillip asked.

Still agitated, she said, "You were happy. Don't you see? That was you, Peppy. You were the one so happy. You can't remember it, but you were. I promise you. Don't you understand? That's what I came here to tell you. That's all. Just that."

"Oh. But what happened then? Did I let Daddy take me out into the water or what?"

Aggie looked up at the window high on the wall. "Nothing. Nothing happened."

"We went home? The picnic was over?"

"No, it—it wasn't over. Not yet."

"We ate then?"

"No, we—we'd already eaten. Momma finished her watermelon."

"I mean, did I go into the water by myself?"

"No, not then. You—you didn't go in then."

"That's the end of the story?"

"That's what I came to tell you. That you were happy. We all were. I wanted you to know that, even if you can't remember it."

"But there must have been other times—times with you and George and Momma and Daddy—"

"No. There were no other times. Not like that." Slowly her eyelids lowered as if she wanted to go to sleep. Then she opened her eyes wide and stood up. "And now that I've told you, I can go." She brushed the front of her skirt as if she'd been eating something with crumbs.

"No other times? Ever?"

"I have to go. I'm sure the time's up." Again she looked at the floor around her chair, around the table and under it, as if she'd misplaced something.

"You looking for something?"

"Nothing. They took my coat and my purse. You could have helped me into it, my coat. You could have handed me my purse. But they took them from me." She brushed her skirt again, then started toward the door.

"Wait," Phillip said. "The back of your sweater, it's bunched up." He went to her and reached toward the sweater.

"No! You mustn't come too close. That's why they took my coat, my purse. For my sake. They did it in mercy, so you wouldn't come too close."

"All right. But your sweater—in back—"

"Momma went swimming out in the middle of the river." Aggie's voice was low, her head slightly bowed. "And Daddy too, the way they always did. George climbed up into the willow tree and I was picking the seeds out of a piece of watermelon and breaking off a chunk for you. Momma yelled 'Arthur' at Daddy—Daddy's name—and then she yelled it again. Daddy yelled her name—'Mary!'—and then, when I looked up, Momma's arm was stuck straight up out of the water and Daddy was swimming out toward her. But she was moving away from him even if her arm was out of the water and she wasn't really swimming. She was caught in the current and had a cramp. 'No, Arthur, no,' she yelled, but Daddy didn't even yell her name back. He kept on swimming toward her. Then he got to where she was, and all I could see was a lot of splashing as if they were having a water fight out there in the river. I could see the splashing move away, down the river, in the current, Momma and Daddy still in the middle of it. George was climbing down from the tree, and I was standing at the river calling Momma and Daddy to come back. Then I jumped in, and George, too, and we started to swim, but when we couldn't see the splashing anymore, we yelled and yelled 'Momma! Daddy!' but we couldn't see the splashing. A boat, a rowboat, came around the tip of the cove, going to where Momma and Daddy had been. We stood up in the water, George and me, and we watched. We shivered because all of a sudden it was cold. The water came up to my chest, up to George's chin. We stood there until we couldn't even see the boat anymore, it was going so fast around the far side of the cove."

With the back of her hand, she wiped her mouth. "When people came to get us, I was putting on your rompers because it was getting dark and we had to go home. And when people came, I started to cry because George wouldn't come down out of the tree so we could go home."

With a sweep of her head, she turned and looked at Phillip. Her eyes were wide, her lips pressed hard together. "That isn't what I came to tell you. Only that you'd been happy. That's why I wanted to come. Forget what I said just now. Please. Remember what I said before." She had begun to plead, the eyes, the mouth exhausted now. "Remember that. Only that. Please!"

Phillip had started to reach a hand toward her, but she flung herself toward the door and beat her fist against it. "Out! Out! Let me—"

Phillip lurched forward, but he had forgotten his leg irons. He stumbled against the side of a chair. "Aggie! Wait!" Down he went, hitting the side of the table, his left foot pinned under his right leg. "I'll go with you. You don't have to go alone." With one hand on the table, the other pushing against the floor tiles, he raised himself. But it was too late. The door was closed. She was gone.

"Aggie? Wait for me," he called.

He was on his feet now, staring at the closed door. He took one step, then another, the leg irons straining as he struggled to lengthen his stride. "You don't have to go all by yourself. I'll go with you. Wait."

NINE

The air was clean and crisp, with a clear sky overhead. Every star was out and Rachel was reminded of what it had been like when, as a girl, she'd gone to midnight Mass on Christmas Eve—this cold, this clean, always. Tonight she had put the lining into her raincoat so she was warm from her knees to her neck, but her overshoes were thin rubber, meant to keep out the wet, not the cold. And the scarf on her head, a silky material with bright purple violets on it, didn't help to warm her ears. She'd chosen mittens instead of gloves, however, so her hands were warm and her fingers too. A thick wheat-colored scarf scratched its heat into her neck, but her nose she could do nothing about. No matter. It was with her nose that she took in the winter air. It was her nose that captured the cold and knew it to be clean and crisp. If she were to cover her nose, she would only dampen the scratchy scarf, and it would keep her from experiencing the stillness, the world cleansed, prepared and waiting for the snow that would surely come soon.

She had told the man who'd driven her here—the same driver who had brought her before and who had almost gotten a speeding ticket, the same man who had taken her to Mrs. McTygue's. She'd told him now to wait until she got back and, please, not to try to say anything to her when he would see her later. Absolutely nothing at all, if he didn't mind. He said he didn't mind and, she'd told him, he must not mention her name to anyone who might come to the car. He was to say he was with Mrs. McTygue. She made him repeat the name three times: Mrs. McTygue. He was with Mrs. McTygue. Under no circumstance should he mention Sister Rachel. For the deception, he was being given a generous sum added to his usual fee, the total expenditure of all her traveling adding up now to the exact amount of the check sent her by Mr. Thomas Tallent in her brother's name so long ago.

The guard station was less then fifty feet away, the lights in the windows yellow, going toward brown, a warmer glow than usual as if it were coming not from electricity, but from candles made of beef tallow. Away from the house, at the far edge of the parking lot, were—as far as Rachel could make out—a small group of people standing in the cold, holding lit candles. Just past them was another group, larger, holding signs. These would be the people who had come to protest or to celebrate her brother's death.

Someone, a man, huddled down into a huge dark coat, was walking toward her. He was going to send her away. He was going to tell her that her deception had been discovered, that she was not Mrs. McTygue, the mother of the murdered prison guard, in spite of the letter in her purse identifying her as such. She was, he would say, Sister Rachel, and her brother Phillip was the condemned murderer. She was therefore ineligible to witness the execution by order of the prison warden.

The man coming toward her had his hands jammed into his coat pockets and was walking with a sway that shoved first one of his shoulders forward, then the other, a display of authority and self-approval. Rachel squeezed her purse in her mittened hands, wishing she could hear the crackle of the letter inside that gave her permission to be there. But she heard nothing even though she knew the letter was inside, that it would identify her, the bearer, as Mrs. McTygue, the bereaved mother, and she would be allowed to proceed, an honored guest.

The letter had been given to Rachel by Mrs. McTygue herself. She, Rachel, had written to her and had asked that she be allowed to come visit her. She'd asked that she be given a chance, in person, to represent her brother's family to the family of the murdered guard, to beg pardon, to make an offering of condolence and a promise of prayer. It seemed the honorable thing to do. Mrs. McTygue, in a note written in perfect Palmer penmanship, had told Rachel that she might come on a Tuesday, at two in the afternoon, and Rachel had gone.

Mrs. McTygue lived in the prison town of Chevaren in a small two-story house surrounded by a lawn and closed in by a metal crosshatched security fence. Taking up most of the front lawn, to the right of the walk-way, was a satellite dish, a huge shallow bowl tipped on its edge with a small truncated cone at its center. Planted around the tipped rim that touched the ground were what looked like the remains of begonia, enshrining the dish, making it seem not a piece of galactic apparatus but a prized sculpture, an honored decoration that gave the lawn and the house itself distinction. Even the staked guy wires that anchored it firmly to the earth—making sure it wouldn't take off in search of its parent satellite—were circled by plants, but she didn't know their names.

The house had no porch. Three cement steps led up to the front door. After Rachel, standing one step lower than the entrance, had rung the bell, a woman opened the door, but only a few inches. The glass storm door remained closed.

"Yes?" Rachel heard the woman say.

"Mrs. McTygue? Sister Rachel. Your letter said I might stop by."

The woman stared a moment, then the door was opened wider, the storm door still kept closed. She was wearing a nubby pink housecoat that zipped up the front and she was fumbling nervously in her pocket. Finally she brought out a rubber band. With both hands—led by the thumbs—she swept above her ears and gathered together the slate-gray hair that had been hanging down to her shoulders. After a few twists of the rubber band, she managed to get the hair tied at the back of her neck, with one wayward strand still straggling over her right ear. The woman then opened the front door all the way, then the storm door, a sufficient indication that Rachel might come in.

Mrs. McTygue was short and stout with blue, almost bulging eyes under which she'd smudged some pale-blue shadow that didn't quite cover the dark gray underneath. Her eyelids were heavy as if exhausted by the repeated chore of covering, then uncovering, eyes so rounded and so large. Lipstick had been streaked across her upper lip, with the lower lip completely bare except for a slight frecklelike mark close to the middle. It could be a fleck of tobacco. She was fumbling again in the pocket of her housecoat, but the pocket seemed empty.

When Rachel stepped into the house, they were immediately in the living room, with no intervening hallway where Rachel might make some quick adjustment to being in this woman's home. What she saw suggested that she had come at the wrong time, that Mrs. McTygue hadn't finished her preparations. Newspapers and magazines were piled, some precariously, on a coffee table, a lamp table, and the top of the television set. On an overstuffed chair were a thick winter coat, dark brown, a blue knit dress, and two sweaters, one of them draped over the back. Unfolded laundry—sheets, undergarments, towels, blouses—were heaped on the couch, and in front of the coffee table was a sausage-shaped vacuum cleaner, its components arranged around it, making it look like an indulged pug-dog surrounded by its toys. On a magazine pile was a porcelain gravy boat with what looked like the remains of cornflakes.

On the television screen two women, one blond, one brunette, were talking in overamplified voices about someone named Kyle. They weren't raising their voices—Mrs. McTygue had done that for them—but there was a finely modulated intensity in what they were saying. A young man joined them, smiling, with what could only be called a warmhearted arrogance. He was wearing a blue blazer, and the two top buttons of his shirt were undone to make room for a silk scarf neatly tied at the base of his neck, probably to indicate that he was unreliable.

Mrs. McTygue was asking Rachel to sit down, without having asked if she would like to take off her coat. When Rachel hesitated, Mrs. McTygue picked up one of the sweaters from the overstuffed chair and put it on the arm of the couch. Rachel sat down, shoving the winter coat and dresses to one side. The coat almost slipped to the floor, but she grabbed it just in time. The dress and the other sweater she bunched up against her, cushioning her side.

Mrs. McTygue told her she was about to make some coffee, or tea if she preferred. Rachel said tea because it would be the easiest to fix. When Mrs. McTygue apologized for not having any milk or sugar in the house, Rachel assured her that she took neither, or, for that matter, she didn't even require the tea if it was any trouble.

"Trouble? Why would anything be any trouble?" The woman seemed genuinely perplexed, so Rachel said nothing. Mrs. McTygue picked up a sauce pan that had been sitting on the coffee table and took it with her when she left the room.

Rachel wondered if she could turn off the television or at least lower the sound, but she considered this presumptuous. The blond had left, and the brunette was now coldly angry with the young man, much to his sleepy-eyed delight.

Rachel pulled the woolen dress out from under her and draped that, too, across the arm of the couch. The laundry, she noticed, had been squashed down in places and, on a dish towel near the arm, there were dirt smudges in two places. Mrs. McTygue would apparently stretch out on the couch, her shoes or slippers on, to watch TV, ignoring the uneven pillowing beneath her. Rachel looked at a pair of pale green slacks at the far end of the couch and thought she might at least replace them with something more comfortable for Mrs. McTygue to use as a head cushion (there was a zipper), but then another idea came to her. She would ask Mrs. McTygue if she could fold her laundry and clean her house. She would ask if she could scrub, vacuum, and dust. She would do that much at least. For Mrs. McTygue.

Rachel was standing, reaching for the green slacks. She would set them aside, along with the other ironing. She would even iron. But before she had touched the slacks, she sat back down. The man and the woman on the TV were flickering next to her right eye, mostly orange and green. The word "Acapulco" was being mentioned, the brunette with derision, the man with low-throated insinuation. Rachel would not fold and iron for Mrs. McTygue, nor would she move the green slacks. She would not scrub, neither would she vacuum and dust. She would sit right where she was. She wouldn't even turn down the TV.

What surrounded her were the artifacts of grief. The senselessness of continued living was declared in all she saw. Despair had left the laundry untended; loss had piled the papers and magazines; the vacuum cleaner was a silent lamentation and the overamplified voices were the sounds of a dirge. No more than Rachel could dismiss Mrs. McTygue's grief, no more than she could erode the despair, could she put the woman's house in order. Grief was chaos, that much Rachel knew. What for some might have been the tearing of hair and the rending of garments was, for Mrs. McTygue, disorder and indifference. Rather than throw herself on the pyre, she would stretch out on the untended clothes.

An automobile commercial had come onto the television, cars screeching, trying to fly out through the screen and crash into the living room. Music played by no known instruments urged them on. Someone was making a speech, inciting the car to louder screeches, more violent dangers. To obliterate the car before it could make its leap into the room, Rachel reached out to the dial, but before she could touch it, the car disappeared and was replaced by a woman in blue jeans and a green sweatshirt. Her shining dark hair was pulled back into a single curl that wound down her back, her face bright with intelligent good will. She was spreading peanut butter onto a slice of bread for a little blond girl standing next to her. She was talking about her determination that the little girl should be kept healthy and satisfied, that she—the little girl— should be denied nothing.

The peanut butter was being expertly spread as if the bread were being decorated like a cake. And the woman, after she'd given the little girl the piece of bread and touched her cheek to send her out to play, ran her finger along the flat side of the knife, gathering the last of the peanut butter. This she licked without putting the finger itself into her mouth.

Mrs. McTygue had come into the room and was standing in front of the TV. She was holding a large leather-covered book. It looked like a Bible. She turned to Rachel and held out the book. "Some pictures you might want to look at. I took most of them." Rachel accepted the book, a photograph album. "I mean, this is why you wanted to come, isn't it? To look at pictures of Donny? I can show you his room, too, if you want."

"The pictures for now. Thank you."

"You can see his room after. He never let me in, but it's all right now. He's gone."

After watching a teenage girl and the brunette on the TV for a moment—they were in a pizza place—Mrs. McTygue gave a sad, disapproving shake of the head at the screen and left. Rachel started to call after her, to tell her she'd come for just a short visit, to talk for a little while. Not even the tea was obligatory. But Mrs. McTygue had disappeared down a hallway to the right of a staircase leading upstairs. There was the slightest swirl of the skirt of her housecoat, the last sight of her, disappearing after Mrs. McTygue herself had gone—and Rachel thought: could that have been the Angel? But it had obviously been Mrs. McTygue. The housecoat was pink and nubby, like a chenille bedspread. This could not have been the Angel. Besides, her cure was passing from her; she must know now that the Angel was never meant to come, that the Angel had never been there to begin with.

Yet Rachel was tempted to hope the opposite. It had been a solace to believe, in her cure, that direct heavenly intervention was imminent. But, Rachel reminded herself, such thoughts, such needs, were caused by her cure. To allow them into her mind now would negate the small advance she had made through the wilderness. If she were to ask for the Angel's return, she might not be allowed to mourn the children, each by name. She would be drawn back even more completely into the uncertainties, the bewilderments that stood between herself and her old sorrows. She must surrender any hope that the Angel might come. She must allow her sorrows to return.

Rachel opened the album about a third of the way through so she wouldn't have to look at the entire book. Studying the pictures would help to steady her. On the TV, the brunette was holding the slice of pizza the teenager was eating. They were giggling. Rachel looked down at the opened book. There was Mrs. McTygue, younger, standing on a sidewalk, wearing a coat with a fur collar. Another picture showed Mrs. McTygue and two other women watching a fourth woman—who was wearing a corsage—open a package the size of a handkerchief box. Mrs. McTygue's hair was longer then, and her face thinner.

On the TV, something had happened while Rachel wasn't looking. The teenager, a daughter probably, was pushing the pizza away from herself. Now the brunette was angry too. Some words about Kyle were spoken, then the brunette burst into tears. The teenager was looking down, sulking, touching the edge of the pizza crust.

Rachel had turned two pages of the album. A brown-haired boy, his pants hitched up halfway to his chest so his ankles were sticking out from the bottom, was squinting into the sun, his nose wrinkled, his mouth twisted in discomfort. Three pages ahead the boy, older, was in a uniform of some kind, a Boy Scout maybe, except he had on a hat with a visor. A military school perhaps. Then here was the boy with Mrs. McTygue and a tall kid with a knobby face. Mr. McTygue? The boy held a broom on his shoulder like a rifle. The man's arm was around the boy's waist; the boy was smiling.

The brunette was alone with the pizza. She wasn't crying anymore. Her lips were pursed; she was fingering the pizza. Like the peanut butter woman, she got some of the tomato sauce on her finger and brought it to her mouth.

"Here's the ones you want to see." Rachel jerked upward. Mrs. McTygue had come back and was blocking the TV. From the music and from the quick colors that flashed out from around Mrs. McTygue, Rachel assumed another car commercial had come on. Mrs. McTygue was bending over her, smelling like vanilla, turning the pages of the album. "I put the water on. But you still have time to see these."

Mrs. McTygue was standing up again. Rachel saw flashes of gray, blue and orange at her sides, with an occasional splash of green. On the album page was a series of pictures, a clown juggling Indian clubs in front of a group of children sitting on the floor. The clown had the expected red nose, the yellow yarn hair, the big, baggy pajamalike suit decorated with huge polka dots like the wrapping for Wonder Bread. A smile like a curved hot dog was painted on his whitened face, his cheeks were dotted with red patches, and a vertical and a horizontal line crossed each of his eyes as if the eyes were targets seen through a gun sight. The children were entranced, staring up at him, their mouths open. There must have been about twenty children, like a kindergarten class. Mrs. McTygue's son must be the clown.

Mrs. McTygue turned the page. The clown was still there, but with different children. There was also a picture of the clown alone, then of the clown with two laughing children, the clown with Mrs. McTygue and, behind them, well-dressed adults with drinks in their hands.

"They loved him. Everybody loved him. Everybody, no matter who. That there, in the suit, that's Hiram Schneider, the mayor. He loved him. You would have too. Look at him." She had turned to other pictures with the Indian clubs and the clown. It was here that Rachel realized that, at any moment, she would be beaten by Mrs. McTygue, the same as she had been beaten by Mrs. Levo. Nothing was happening that told her this, unless it was Mrs. McTygue's growing passion about the love for her son. It had been that way with Mrs. Levo, except that with Mrs. Levo Rachel didn't know it was about to happen.

Mrs. Levo, too, had had a vacuum cleaner and a television. There, too, had been the picture album. Mrs. Levo was mother of Anthony, one of the children killed in the fire. In the painting on the refectory wall, Anthony was sitting in the lower right-hand corner eating a salami sandwich on thick homemade bread. Mrs. Levo was the last of the parents Rachel had gone to visit after the fire, and it was only a few hours later that Rachel was found in the gutted school with her veil ripped away and her clothing torn. But Mrs. Levo had not ripped the veil nor torn the clothing. She had only struck her. Rachel had done the rest herself. Mrs. Levo had only slapped her, then landed her fist against Rachel's eye, the ring on her finger cutting into the skin all the way down to Rachel's mouth. Rachel had grabbed Mrs. Levo just below the shoulders, but the woman's fists beat against the starched wimple at her chest, then at her arms, her neck, her back to the right of her spine. Just as Sister Annette, who had been with Mrs. Levo's little girl, Carla, in her room upstairs looking at her toys, came into the room, Mrs. Levo had thrown Rachel to the floor, skinning her face along the rough carpet. The woman quickly covered her face with her hands, a streak of blood trickling down her ring finger where she'd cut Rachel's lip. While Carla stared, Sister Annette had helped Rachel to her feet. Mrs. Levo had kept her hands in front of her face.

Mrs. McTygue stood up straight again and the colors from the TV—now dark blue and green, with some white and some brown—flashed out from behind her as if she were radioactive. Rachel looked at the rapt, upturned faces of the children. It seemed to her now that the juggling itself was not entertainment, but a summoning of wonders yet to come. It was a form of conjuring. At any moment, the hoped-for splendor might appear if only the clown could persist in his invocation.

The clown himself seemed in near-stupefied terror, unbreathing, struggling not to look at the Indian clubs twirling in front of him. If he were to breathe, the clubs would fall, the children would be bereft, the promised exultation canceled until another time. Again and again, in picture after picture, the juggled clubs seemed to be sent aloft, each a plea, the swift brush against the air, the whispered call that would bring forth the awaited miracle. The clown was faithful even in his terror.

"See how everybody loved him? Children, old people, the mayor. Do you see it?"

Rachel turned the page, eager to witness the clown's success, the great splash of summoned glory that would change the children's fear to

154

joy, and transform the clown himself from suppliant to triumphant priest. But the page was empty. There were no more pictures. Rachel looked down at the blank paper. Slowly she drew her fingers across its surface, feeling the rough texture against her flesh. When she reached the bottom corner of the page, she stopped.

"Can you see it? Tell me! How everybody loved him?"

"Yes," Rachel said quietly. "I can see that." Neither woman moved.

In the kitchen, the teakettle continued to shriek, the sound trying to pierce the barrier beyond which it could escape from human hearing. On the television, the peanut butter lady had returned, and it seemed that it was from her kitchen that the screeching came, that behind the smooth words was a prolonged cry, begging her to stop. The lady was lathering the bread, efficient, expert, ignoring the scream coming from somewhere over her shoulder.

Rachel moved toward the door. She would give Mrs. McTygue no chance to beat her. Mrs. McTygue started after her. "Wait," she said. Rachel touched the doorknob, then took her hand away.

Mrs. McTygue came no closer. She had put down the album and was crushing something in her housecoat pocket. She brought out a white envelope. "You go," she said, shouting over the kettle's whistle. "You saw how everybody loved him. So *you* go! It would be better than me going. This will let you in. *You* watch! *You* see what it's like! That's what I *really* want. *That's* why I let you come!" She shoved the envelope against Rachel's chest, crushing it against the top button of her coat. Mrs. McTygue took her hand away. Rachel caught the envelope before it could fall.

Mrs. McTygue herself opened the door, first turning the knob the wrong way, then the right way. Framed in the doorway they both stood in the cold, the kettle's whistle now a winter wind wailing around the TV dish on the other side of the security fence. "Will you go? To see it when it happens to your brother?"

Rachel wetted her lips, preparing to say something, but before the words could be spoken, Mrs. McTygue had slammed the door. The teakettle could still be heard. There was a slight thrum from one of the guy wires tethering the dish.

The dark figure walking toward Rachel from the guardhouse was holding out an ungloved hand. Rachel had stopped walking, waiting for the man to come nearer. "Mrs. McTygue, good evening. I'm Bob Reynolds. Warden Buckley told you I'd be here, I believe. Let's go inside where it's nice and cozy." They started to shake hands, but Rachel remembered her mitten. She pulled it off, and they finally shook. Mr. Reynolds' hand was warm and slightly damp. "If there's anything in particular I can do for you, please don't hesitate. All right?"

He took Rachel by the lower arm and steered her toward the doorway and the yellow-lighted window. "There is one thing," Rachel said. "If it can be arranged."

"Just ask."

"I would like to see Mr. Manrahan."

Through the window Rachel saw a uniformed guard sipping something from a thick white mug. When he took the mug away, she saw that he had soaked the hair of his bushy black moustache.

TEN

Phillip watched the capful of honey-colored detergent flow smoothly down into the water on top of his socks. It was like pouring olive oil onto a salad. He rinsed the cap under the faucet to make sure he got the full benefit of the detergent and placed the cap— a nice bright red—on the shelf next to the sink. Being executed had its advantages. He'd asked for some Arm & Hammer laundry detergent to replace the sand-gritted black soap he'd had to use before, and lo, it had been given to him. He'd also asked for some brown shoe polish, and that, too, had been given. It was his plan to let the socks soak while he polished his shoes, then, by washing out his socks, he would clean his hands of the shoe polish. In other times, he had found it helpful to wash his hair after shining his shoes. It cleaned the shoe polish from his hands, and from under his fingernails as well. But since he wouldn't have a chance to shower after the shoeshine, he thought of the sock washing as his last official act, after he'd polished his shoes. At least he'd present himself to the assembled with clean fingernails.

It had not been easy, deciding what he would do to fill the last hour or so before his dying. Like any traveler preparing for a journey, he wanted to be ready in time, not just with everything neatly packed, but with his house in order and the timely completion of all the scheduled tasks that would allow an easy departure. Of course, he'd worried that all his chores might be done, his preparations accomplished—and there would still be time left to fill. He would be stuck, waiting, with nothing to do.

Phillip squashed the socks down into the sink, the suds bursting between his fingers. Since he'd been instructed to wear no socks—there would be straps around his ankles—he would be able to wash all four pair, leaving behind him a sweet-smelling legacy that he would let dry along the edge of his shelf, like Christmas stockings ready for Santa Claus. There would be eight socks, a fair-sized family, surely deserving of Christmas bounty.

Then, too, Phillip had a second reason for concentrating on his socks and shoes. He had been asked a few moments earlier, by Quinn, the head guard that night, if he would agree to see Mrs. McTygue, the mother of the man he'd killed. She had come to watch the execution and had asked for a brief interview. It would have been cowardly to refuse and, besides, the authorities had so readily given him the detergent and the shoe polish that he felt himself somewhat in their debt. Yes, he would see Mrs. McTygue. But Mrs. McTygue must excuse him if he went about his chores. He had things to do, and they could not be postponed.

Phillip held the socks down at the bottom of the sink. The water was warm and smooth against his wrists. He deliberately raised and lowered his hands, taking them out of the water, pushing them back in, feeling the soothing warmth. He heard the suds crinkle and explode against his wrists like the snap, crackle, and pop of Rice Krispies.

When he raised his hands again, the bolt slipped back, and the puff of air indicated that the cell door would open. Mrs. McTygue had arrived. Phillip thought the entire interview could pass with him standing at the sink. He might not even turn around. He would let the woman say what she had come to say without facing her. But that would be rude, and he had no reason to be rude to this woman.

"This is Mrs. McTygue. You said it was all right she could come." It was Quinn's voice and in it was a note of quiet warning that Phillip behave himself—although Quinn would be sore pressed to come up with a suitable punishment at a time like this, should Phillip disobey.

"Yes," Phillip said. "It's all right." To throw off the soapsuds, he shook his hands loosely over the sink, then wiped them on his pants, twice, palms and backs, as if he were honing a razor. He turned to face Mrs. McTygue.

Aggie was standing next to Quinn. She was clutching a small brown purse to her waist as if it were her lunch in a paper bag and she was afraid someone might take it from her. Before Phillip could speak her name, she said, "Mr. Manrahan, I'm Mrs. McTygue. Thank you for letting me see you. I consider it a great kindness, especially since we've never met before. Perhaps Mr. Quinn here would allow me just a few moments, alone, if you yourself, Mr. Manrahan, agree."

Phillip shifted his glance sideways, at Quinn, and nodded his head yes, one abrupt nod. "I'm sorry," Quinn said, "but I have to be present at all times. No one except an authorized member of the clergy is allowed alone."

"I see," Aggie said. "All right then. Whatever you say, Officer." Quinn clasped his hands behind him and fixed his gaze on the opposite wall, just above the shelf where Phillip planned to hang out his socks.

"Would you like to sit down, Mrs. McTygue?" Phillip motioned toward the bunk. Aggie turned toward Quinn. "May I sit down, Officer?"

"Sit down is all right. Just you can't touch the prisoner and the prisoner can't touch you. Anything else is permissible." Quinn made his recitation without taking his eyes from the wall, but when he finished, he craned his neck a little as if his shirt collar was too tight.

Aggie sat down on the bunk, still clutching the purse. "Thank you," she said. "Thank you both." She brought her feet back under the bunk, not to make herself comfortable, but, it seemed, to hide her oversize rubber boots. She'd always been conscious of her big feet, and the boots made them look bigger than ever. When she didn't say anything, Phillip shifted his weight from one side to the other to remind her that he was still there. She continued to stare at Quinn; Quinn continued to stare at the wall. "I was washing my socks," Phillip said. "Then I wanted to shine my shoes."

"Yes. Of course. You mustn't let me stop you."

Phillip could, of course, with a word, end the entire scene. All he had to do was call this woman "Aggie." It would let Quinn know she was his sister. The immediate family was not allowed. Aggie would be forced to leave.

Phillip had an image of his sister receding down the prison corridor, Quinn and another guard escorting her. There would be no protest, no pleading, no resistance. She would calmly do as she was told. Her purse would still be clutched at her waist, but more tightly than before. Her head would be lifted, her feet light against the corridor stones. She would accept her brother's betrayal; she would go out into the night uncomplaining and alone.

"I'll just let my socks soak then," he said, "while I shine my shoes. I hope you don't mind if I go ahead with what I'd planned to do."

"Not at all. Go right ahead, Mr. Manrahan. Don't let me interrupt."

"Thanks." Phillip went to the wall opposite the sink where he'd set out his shoes, the polish and, for a polishing rag, his washcloth since he wouldn't need it anymore. He had thought of using a sleeve of his sweatshirt but decided it was still in good shape and could go to someone else now that the weather had turned so cold. He settled down on his haunches and began dusting his right shoe with the washcloth, getting it ready for the polish.

With a corner of the cloth, he applied the polish to the toe of the shoe, rubbing it in, using circular motions. Aggie said nothing. Phillip, his head bent over the shoe, was smoothing the polish along the edge of the sole when he saw Aggie stand up and go to the sink. She began washing the socks, scrubbing a green one against a brown, her head pulled back to escape any splashing.

Phillip daubed the polish onto his left shoe, rubbing it in, smoothing it along the sides, using his forefinger to get it in along the instep. He made the small circular motions that would rub the polish well down into the leather.

Aggie slopped the socks in and out of the water. She had said nothing. She began wringing out two of the socks, a dark brown one and a navy blue, twisting them into each other, letting the water run back into the sink. Phillip buffed the toe of his right shoe.

Fresh water was running into the sink. Aggie was rinsing the socks, forcing them down into the fresh water, allowing them to swell, then squooshing them so the water would rush through the wool, taking with it the soap. Now she was examining the heel of a maroon sock as if trying to decipher the secrets of its weave.

Phillip watched a moment, then said quietly, "I have a sister who can paint. Pictures, I mean. Not a lot of people have heard of her, but she's a great, great painter. When we were children, she let me help her paint lilac bushes on the side of the garage in our backyard. We didn't have any money for paint, so she'd pester housepainters for what was left over, or for their empty cans so she could scrape out what was left even if it was only enough for a leaf or part of a branch of the lilac bushes.

"It took all summer practically, not because my sister was lazy, but because there would be times when no one was painting a house. When she got more green than blue, the bushes had more leaves than lilacs, and some of the lilacs had to be white because she got a lot of white. When some red paint turned up, she used that for the background, for the sky really, saying it was sunset so the red wouldn't be wasted.

"I painted mostly what would be grass growing at the bottom of the lilac bushes because I was so much smaller than she was, but she let me. Some of the grass had to be yellow because she got herself half a can. She said it hadn't rained so the grass was turning yellow. When it was all finished, two days before school started—I was going into morning kindergarten—the side of the garage was covered with lilac bushes. My sister, because I'd helped, bought us a twin Popsicle, orange, so we could eat it 'under the lilac bushes,' she said. She got half and I got the other half, and we sat there leaning against the side of the garage, licking our

Popsicles. We forgot that some of the paint wasn't dry yet. I had green and yellow all over the back of my shirt and some green in my hair. My sister, because she was taller, had blue in her hair. When she found out what had happened, she said, 'Look! I've got lilacs in my hair!' " His voice broke and he stopped.

Aggie shoved the socks back down into the water and began moving her hand around and around to create a whirlpool. Some water splashed over the side. She pulled back quickly, and the water landed on the floor. Now the water was being sucked down into the drain. Fresh water was pouring into the sink. The socks were being kneaded. From the motions of her arms, Aggie could be working with dough. Down she pushed, then relented, then down again, then another release.

Aggie took two of the socks into her cupped hands and pressed them together, letting the water run back into the sink. Then she set them on top of the toilet tank, gently, as if afraid to make any noise. "I have a brother," she said quietly, "and it would seem that he will leave this world before I do and what will happen to him I don't really know. And yet I'll tell you this—"

The bolt clanged; the air was released and the door slid open. Officer Quinn walked over to Aggie, but she kept right on talking. "I will tell you this: that when my own time comes, if my brother does not greet me at heaven's gate, I will not enter. If he is not the one—"

"I'm sorry," Officer Quinn said. "But time is up, Mrs. McTygue. It's rules and we have to be very strict."

"—If he is not the one to lead me into the company of angels and of saints I will not go. If it is not at my brother's side that I approach the throne of mercy, I will walk the other way and never return."

A man in a heavy overcoat had come into the cell, just inside the door. Aggie reached her hand toward the sink, toward the socks.

"Mrs. McTygue?" the man in the overcoat said. Aggie brought her hand up to her throat. Water dripped down onto the front of her raincoat and soaked into the scarf just beneath her chin. Without looking at Phillip she said, "To all of this I have sworn, and against it nothing will prevail. Ever." She then let herself be taken by the elbow and led toward the door of the cell. The door closed behind her, this time without the usual clang to punctuate the pneumatic poof.

Phillip had put on the finely polished shoes and was finishing the socks, wringing them out. The bolt slipped quietly back and the door opened. There was a slight scuffling behind him. When Phillip turned, Quinn was trying to push the other guard, Cuppernall, in ahead of him, and Cuppernall was trying to get Quinn to go in first. Phillip stepped back from the sink. The two guards entered, Quinn first, then Cuppernall. Phillip hadn't hung up the socks to dry. His hands were still stained with brown shoe polish. And his fingernails hadn't gotten clean.

ELEVEN

M r. Reynolds, the prosecutor, and the warden, Mr. Buckley, were shaking hands. Then the doctor in attendance, a Dr. Thrale, and Mr. Reynolds were shaking hands. Then each in turn—the warden, the doctor, and the prosecutor, again—shook Rachel's hand. Mr. Buckley was what people call "portly"—which meant he carried his big stomach extremely well. He was wearing rimless eyeglasses and a flowered tie, anemones it seemed. Dr. Thrale was "robust"—which meant he was about to become fat all over. He, too, wore a tie, but a bow tie, navy blue with little white spots called "dotted Swiss." His color was "swarthy"— which meant he drank too much or had high blood pressure. Mr. Reynolds, on the other hand, was simply lean now that he had taken off his winter coat. The lower button of his gray suit jacket was loose and dangled down playfully. He wore a narrow red knit tie that seemed pulled inward so it could lie along the concavity of the man's consumptive chest. Rachel felt relieved that she was wearing the dark blue dress that was her part of the legacy left behind by the Mother General. (She had to let down the hem, but the rest fit fine.) Getting dressed earlier she had been afraid that the dress was too formal—she was wearing it because it was wool—

but she needn't have worried. This was a formal event, a ceremony of state, and one should, out of respect, dress accordingly.

They continued down the corridor and past a paneled screen. It was made of stretched cloth, like heavy linen, and could be part of a stage set, although the play it served would have to be rather bland if the pale-green color was any indication.

With Mr. Reynolds at her elbow, Rachel stepped into a room that looked like an amphitheater, but in miniature. There were three curved banks of benches rising in a near semicircle from a cleared area to the back wall. Porcelain tiles, thicker than the ones in Peppy's cell, lined the walls to within three feet of the high ceiling. Two dim bulbs put a gray shadow over the bench area; Rachel felt she was entering a neutral territory in which no one and nothing had yet been clearly defined.

Mr. Reynolds steered her into the second row where, at the far end, two men with their coats still on, were talking in hushed voices, their heads bent. The third row was almost filled, mostly with men, though two women were among them, one wearing a gray felt hat like a man's. At the far end, all by himself, was a little man, dark-skinned—Indian or Pakistani, Rachel guessed—in a black suit and a white shirt open at the collar. He was sitting up very straight. His eyes were large and dark and under them were smudges as if the man hadn't slept for quite some time. It could be a trick of the light and the shadow, but there seemed to be tears on his cheeks and in his large round eyes.

A woman with straight blond hair sat in the first row, next to Dr. Thrale. She had a small paper pad—pale pink—held to her lower thigh by the lightest touch of her long, slender fingers, and a black Bic pen. The doctor folded his hands in his lap, ready for the play to begin. He twitched his head sideways, then managed to hold it still. The woman, with the index finger of her free hand, rubbed delicately along her lips to smooth her lipstick.

In a clearing at the foot of the tiers, one huge bulb, unfrosted, hung from a single wire over an outsize chair. The chair, back near the far wall, was made of four-by-fours and six-inch planks; the wood seemed raw but worn down, like the lumber her brother George had salvaged when the Wixteds' garage was torn down and he built a fence between their yard and the Schlicks' so she could plant hollyhocks along it. ("To plant hollyhocks," she'd said, "you have to have a fence first.") The chair, however, could be the throne for an ancient king, a prop for some primitive play in which a mad tyrant would make terrible pronouncements and issue malevolent decrees.

Then Rachel noticed the wide leather belts, like the ones worn by motorcycle riders, attached to the arms and to a metal block placed under the seat. There was also a strap across the middle slat of the chair and, hanging just a little lower than the light bulb, suspended on thick wires, was what appeared to be a leather ski mask, except there were no holes for the eyes, only for the nose and mouth. It resembled a dead spider, hung from a taut strand of its own web.

Rachel looked at the chair, at the wires and straps. She couldn't help remembering—however vaguely—the apparatus of her cure. There, in the hospital, next to a high, narrow bed, had been what seemed to be a radio, a Philco, a table model common in those days, in the shape of a rounded arc like the top of a church window to make it look streamlined and modern. It had dials, just like a radio, and little recessed windows where, with thin lines and numbers, the several stations could no doubt be located. Someone would probably turn the dials, moving the pointed needle to the desired number, and they would be given the appropriate program: music, a voice talking, someone singing, or actors acting out a story. Or so it had seemed to Rachel when she'd been brought into the room for the first of many treatments.

Next to the bed there had been a man in a white smock, the kind of smock Rachel wore when she painted. He would be the one to turn on the radio, the one who knew best which program would cure Rachel of her illness. There were straps on the bed—to protect her, the nurse said, to make sure she wouldn't fall. Into Rachel's mouth the nurse put what seemed the upper plate of her grandmother's false teeth—except it had no actual teeth, just the gums. It would protect Rachel's tongue, she was told. It calmed Rachel to see how protective they were all being. Wires with little metal plugs at the ends were then attached to her temples with something sticky, gray, and translucent, like spit. It had made Rachel curious when the plugs weren't put into her ears. How could she hear the radio if the plugs weren't in her ears?

Before she could ask, the man was reaching toward the dial. She couldn't remember which way he turned it, nor could she remember which program he'd tuned into. She could remember only that the paste sticking the plugs to her head smelled like raspberries, as if the person whose spit they were using had been eating raspberries and cream for breakfast.

The warden, Mr. Buckley, was now telling Rachel that if she had the least inclination to change her mind, she had only to say the word. He would understand. (This had something to do with her being a woman.) But he was, at the same time, proud of her determination to be there. (This also had something to do with her being a woman.) And he was sorry, so sorry, that her son had been martyred because of his dedication to justice and to the law.

Rachel could tell that the man considered the guard's murder a necessary evil so that a bigger purpose could be served. The execution would be the ultimate exercise of justice, and anyone who had made so supreme a sacrifice so that it could take place would, quite naturally, be a hero, a martyr, a man made worthy and good by his contribution to the triumph about to take place.

Rachel and Mr. Reynolds sat down on the bench. It was wooden, painted white like a church pew, with a slightly curved back and not uncomfortable. There was still a certain amount of foot shuffling and elbow knocking against the backs of the benches as the other spectators adjusted themselves in their seats.

"Do you want to take off your coat?" Mr. Reynolds reached across her shoulders.

"On. I'll keep it on," Rachel said. Mr. Reynolds shifted in his seat, preparing for the play about to take place.

The scrapings, the shufflings, the knockings ended; there was one last shoe kicking against the back of a bench, then it was quiet except for a slight wind blowing. Above the great wooden chair, coming down through the ceiling, was a metal duct, screened at the mouth. It was from there that the sound of the breeze came. Rachel breathed in, deep, to see if she might catch some hint of the crisp air in the night outside, but all she could smell was warm dust.

Mr. Reynolds leaned forward, listening, one ear turned toward the chair. Rachel now saw, in the shadow, to the side of the chair, an elderly man wearing a light blue sweater. He was thick at the waist, then his torso narrowed upward to sloping shoulders. The wisps of gray hair on his head were mussed, with some clusters standing straight up, making little tepees on the top of his balding scalp. His hands were in his pockets.

Mr. Buckley adjusted his glasses, and, as if this had been a signal, the two dim overhead bulbs went out, leaving the benches completely in the dark. The man in the blue sweater stepped or, rather, slid sideways, into a little closet off to the right. Out in the corridor, there were scraping sounds and the rattle of wood. The screen was being removed. Then another sound, shuffling, like a measured beat leading into a soft-shoe dance. The bench behind her creaked, then another, then there was absolute silence. Rachel thought she heard cloth whisking against cloth. Then came a ripping sound, quick, a heavy seam being torn. It came again, but stopped before she could be sure she'd heard it.

Phillip came through the bright rectangle of the door. Slightly behind him were two guards, neither touching him, both, it seemed, careful not to crowd him. The seams of his pants legs had been slit to the knee and the loose cloth flapped as he walked. He wore no socks, and his scrubbed anklebones were shiny. He had on his polished brown shoes. His shoelaces were untied, and, without the protective socks, it seemed he would soon have blisters on his heel. She had forgotten how tall he was and how prominent his Adam's apple.

Phillip walked in the direction of the chair. He held his head a little to the side as if he wanted to deflate the ceremonial nature of the event.

169

Under the solitary light, he looked like someone about to be inducted into an important office, a man summoned to high service, about to accept, reluctantly, the honors soon to be bestowed.

The warden stood up, as if in respect, and walked just to the left of the guards. Phillip's back was to the room. With one hand he reached out and touched the arm of the chair, then moved the hand across the seat and let it touch the other arm. He seemed about to turn around and hoist himself onto the chair when the warden said quietly, "Is there anything, Phillip Manrahan, that you would like to say?"

Phillip began to shake his head no, but stopped. Without turning around, he mumbled something. Then he coughed, cleared his throat, and said, his voice low but clear, "Let there be no fire. Let the children not die. Let them live."

Rachel stiffened, but made no sound. Phillip turned halfway toward the room and added, "And let them escape after the baseball game, Butte and Folger. Let them get away and not be caught. Let them go free." He paused, then added, "And let his father not throw the scalding soup." He swallowed, then said, "Amen."

In a whisper, not really wanting to be heard, Rachel said, "And may the guard, Oh God, may the guard, may Officer McTygue not be killed."

Phillip drew in a quick breath and held it. Rachel stared directly at him, but knew she could not be seen.

"Mrs. McTygue!" It was the warden who spoke. "I understand. Believe me, I do. But please, there can be no interruptions."

Phillip, his voice more quiet now, said, "Amen to your prayer then, dear Aggie, and let it all end with that at last."

Quickly his gaze at her was broken as the guards, at an impatient nod from the warden, stepped closer and lifted Phillip onto the chair, shoving him back as far into the seat as he could go. There was a thump, the rattle of buckles, and the slapping of leather. The wide belt was brought across Phillip's chest and fastened at the second hole. The wrists, the calves of his legs, were strapped. Both guards reached at the same time for the mask, then each gestured toward the other, deferring the honor. After one made a slight twitch but stopped, the other took hold of the mask and brought it down over Phillip's head, forcing some of his hair into his eyes. Now only his mouth and his nose were visible, his nostrils expanding and contracting as if he were trying to exercise the muscles.

Mr. Buckley made a slow movement with his right hand, as if he were going to scratch his ear but had changed his mind. There was a loud clunk, solid metal clamped into solid metal, like the closing of a trap. A whine could be heard, like a telegraph wire used to sound when Rachel was a girl. Phillip's head jerked back, and his body was flung forward against the strap belted across his chest. Smoke began to leak out from under the head mask. The feet tried to lift themselves from the floor but were unable. The torso, convulsed now, twisted and heaved as if it were being lashed by a whip.

Rachel could only stare, transfixed. Phillip's lips had become a bright red, straining against the casing of their flesh. As Rachel watched, the lips turned to blue, going toward black, and seemed about to burst wide open. The backs of his hands, the length of his lower arms, had sweat dampening the thick hairs, the water soaking them, running between them.

Stirring in Rachel's gullet was a rising scream; it tickled against the sides of her throat. Now it had become a jabbing, a piercing into the inner flesh, climbing up toward her mouth. She must not scream. To scream would make herself open to possession by madness again. In the moment of abandon, during the unguarded second of her surrender to the scream, terror would grab at her and begin to devour her again. The struggle to escape would be the madness itself come back. To protect herself, she would have to flee; only insanity could save her.

She wanted to scream. She wanted to be saved. But she must not retreat into her insanity even if that was her only safety now. She must not leave her brother all alone. She must be with him—and watch. To fly off into her madness would be to abandon him.

But the scream still grew inside her; it was behind her eyes, under the bones of her cheeks. It was sucking in the walls of her throat, then bloating them outward again, beating against the lymph glands beneath the bones of her jaw. The scream had received the support of her stomach, the encouragement of her chest. But she would not scream. She would not go mad, not again. She had not come to see her brother punished. She had come to declare that he was not abandoned at the last, that she would never abandon him again.

The scream now was in her ears, growing. It was swelling her brain, reverberating along the inside of her skull. It was thrumming the cartilage of her nose and stiffening her tongue.

Smoke crept out from the weave of Phillip's shirt, below the chest and along the shoulders. Her brother's ankles, now cherry red, had begun to swell. Then, as if his neck had been deliberately broken, his head snapped forward, the chin knocked against the chest, bouncing before it lay still. A thin red line of blood began to run zigzag down the left side of his shirt like collected raindrops on a windowpane. The red of the hands, the legs, and the ankles was turning black. More smoke was rising out from around the leather straps as if it were being squeezed out of his pores. There was a "plup" sound, then a quick hiss. The mask just below his forehead had bulged out, then been sucked inward. His eyes seemed to have exploded in his head.

Rachel continued to watch. There was a loud clap, and all sounds stopped except for the light breeze blowing. The last wisps of smoke were drawn upward into the mouth of the metal duct. Rachel sat upright against the back of the bench, her hands open on her lap, arms up, as if to show that there was nothing there, that she had nothing left to offer.

Dr. Thrale was leaning over Phillip, Mr. Buckley watching, curious. The man in the light blue sweater slipped out from behind the partition. He, too, watched the doctor, waiting.

Dr. Thrale straightened up. He had in his hand the coils of a stethoscope. "This man is dead," he said. Mr. Buckley relaxed; the blue-sweatered man put his hands back into his pockets. The woman in the first row glanced at her watch and scribbled something onto her pad. The pen slid off the side of the page and dropped to the floor. The woman sat there, not bothering to reach for it.

Four guards had placed themselves in front of Phillip, looking outward into the room, shielding the body. Rachel could see, between the legs of the third guard, her brother's blackened ankle.

TWELVE

I t had snowed all night, and it was still snowing. There had been some worry that the road winding down from the Motherhouse would not be cleared in time, that the planes and buses scheduled to take the six remaining sisters to their far-flung destinations would be missed, and that Rachel herself would be late for her appointed arrival at the bishop's residence. But the plow had come through half an hour before, banking the snow higher than anyone's head, even Rachel's, and Rachel, with Sister Felicity's help, had shoveled the walkway from the front door down to the drive that led to the road along the river.

Since the death of Sister Rachel's brother a few weeks before, the sisters had been worried, then surprised, then bewildered by the change in their colleague. It was not what they had feared, not what they had expected. At the funeral for her brother, and at the burial—all the sisters had traveled with her to her hometown—she had been almost silent, but quietly efficient. At the requiem Mass, it was Rachel who had chosen the readings, then she herself had read the Epistle of Saint Paul to the Corinthians, ". . . if I have not charity. . . ." Her voice had been gentle, but firm. At the grave—next to the graves of her mother and father and her grandparents, and a memorial stone for her brother George, killed in the war—she had been quietly thoughtful. No tears had been shed; she had simply looked long at the coffin, at the open grave, then led them all away before the lowering.

At the Motherhouse it had been Rachel who had made the final arrangements for the closing of the house and the departures of the remaining sisters. Plane tickets, bus tickets, the actual date of their dispersal, all were taken care of by Sister Rachel. To Sister Agatha it seemed that she had, without specific designation, and without fuss or feathers, assumed the role of Mother General. (This was where their surprise had turned to bewildered acceptance.) Sister Agatha speculated that it might have been because Rachel was with the Mother General at her death. Sister Martha, however, mentioned that Sister Rachel, before her illness and her cure, had often been considered a woman of great promise, destined to become, in the future, the head of the Order. And now, in its own way, it all had come to pass—but by what quiet unnoted process, no one was ever quite sure.

Although the plow had come in time for them to leave, it had come too late for Father Laughlin to make it up the hill for morning Mass. And the phones were out, so they had heard nothing. At first, this had caused some distress. Today's Mass would be the last celebrated in the Mother-house, the last the sisters would participate in as members of their Order. But a solution presented itself when the proper moment came.

All six sisters had arrived in the chapel at seven o'clock that morning. After about ten minutes of silent prayer, when no move had been made to start the service, Rachel stood up and began singing the opening hymn they'd chosen, "Come Holy Ghost, Creator Blest." Before she had reached the middle of the first phrase, the other sisters had stood to take up the song. "And in our hearts take up thy rest. . . ." After the hymn, there was some hesitation before Sister Cathrael continued the liturgy with the *Kyrie*, the plea for mercy, but the sisters paused not at all before singing out the "*Gloria*," the good news first heard by the shepherds on the hills of Bethlehem. When that had ended, no one seemed ready to read the opening prayer from the great red missal, the official book of prayers and rubrics. That was for the priest to read, and there was no priest. When the pause extended itself into restlessness, Rachel stepped forward and dutifully read the prayer. The biblical readings from Ecclesiastes—reminding them that "to every thing there is a season"—the singing of the Psalm—"This is a day which the Lord has made; let us rejoice and be glad"—and the reading, again from Saint Paul's letter to the Corinthians—"if I have not charity"—all these had already been agreed on: Sister Martha to read from Ecclesiastes, Sister Felicty the Psalm, and Sister Cathrael from Saint Paul.

Then came another pause. The time had come for the gospel. It should be read by the presiding priest or an ordained deacon. But Father Laughlin still had not arrived, and any woman called by the Holy Spirit to the diaconate—or to the priesthood for that matter—had been refused. Again Rachel ended the pause. She went to the lectern and read out the gospel of Luke, Chapter One, not only the verses twenty-six through thirty-eight, which recorded, of course, the Annunciation, the historical moment that had given inspiration to the Order, but on past the thirty-ninth verse right through the fifty-sixth, telling of Mary's visit to her cousin, Elizabeth, when, with the words of the announcing angel still thrilling through her blood, she made her great proclamation, the "*Magnificat*," the hymn of acceptance and joy—"My soul gives glory to the Lord and my spirit rejoices in God my Savior." The sisters, as Rachel read, stood transfixed at the trusting and familiar words.

Rachel, as if inspired by the miracle celebrated in the prayer, said, "There will be no homily, no sermon. We have understood these words in our hearts, and in our souls." No one objected. Rachel intoned the Latin hymn they'd chosen for the Offertory, *"Panis Angelicus"*—"Bread of Angels"—then lowered her head and clasped her hands in front of her. Before the song was over, there was the scraping of a few chairs, then the soft movement of feet. Sister Felicity and Sister Martha brought up the bread and wine. They held them out to Rachel. Their faces were quietly commanding even as they continued their singing. Rachel looked first at them, then at the bread—a flat round loaf, whole wheat, that Sister Martha had baked—and at the small flask of red wine. Again she bowed her head and stood unmoving. After a moment, she unclasped her hands, reached out, accepted the offered bread, the flagon of wine.

She put the bread and the wine on the altar table. When the hymn was finished, she said, "We have no ordained priest with us this morning. We could end our final hours together with prayer and with reading the inspired word of God, and this would no doubt be pleasing to our Savior. We could, in humility, accept the loss of final celebration, of one last sharing of the holy sacrifice that is the Mass—and God, we know, would compensate for our loss with special blessings of his own. But it would not be right, it would not be just if we were to part from each other without first participating in the divine sacrifice itself, without taking into our own bodies and into our own blood the body of Christ and the blood of Christ. We are women who have sacrificed our lives to God's service. We have given our bodies and our blood to him. We must not refuse his gift to us, the gift of himself, anymore than he has refused the gift we have given him, the gift of ourselves. We must, before we are dispersed, celebrate the true Mass. We must, through God's grace, join our sacrifice with his, bread and body, body and bread, body and body."

She paused. No one moved. "Then today," she continued, "we are, of necessity, the early church again, before the separation of male and female, when it was recognized that all power came from our baptism, through Jesus Christ. Claiming unity with that time, we will, with all reverence and humility, continue our celebration. If any of you would prefer not to participate, you may leave—with our plea that you pray for us." Again, no one moved.

After that, there were no more pauses, no more hesitations. Rachel proceeded through the sacred sacrifice, simply, quietly, and the gathered sisters participated and responded with growing vigor and a deepening reverence, with Sister Felicity louder, more firm than all the rest. Rachel consecrated the bread and the wine, now the body and blood of the Savior. She held them out, in turn, toward her congregants, and they looked on in silent wonder at what God had achieved.

Breakfast was in the refectory instead of the small servants' dining room they'd been using for their daily meals. The heat had already been turned off in anticipation of their departure, but a fire had been built in the fireplace along the wall nearest the pantry. For fuel, Sister Cathrael had reduced to kindling some broken chairs from the attic, and Sister Martha had ripped out a small cupboard from the kitchen. The cupboard had held breakfast cereal, rice, and spices. Beyond today, it had no purpose. The smell of burning paint from the cupboard wood, white enamel especially, was a bit oversweet, but the scent of coffee and pancakes helped overcome whatever might offend.

Rachel, when she came into the refectory, turned a moment toward the fire and stared into the flames. Sister Agatha, already seated, shifted in her chair but didn't get up. She only watched. Rachel turned away and took her place next to Sister Cathrael. Grace was said, and the eating and the chatter began. The fire popped and sputtered. When the burning wood collapsed into itself, sending sparks up the chimney, Rachel stared again for a long moment, then went back to her pancakes.

Sister Agatha was the first to notice the change in the painting. She had lifted her head to show approval of the coffee and was murmuring a loud *Hmmmm. . . .* There, in the lower left-hand corner of the mural, was a cat. It was gray, sitting on its haunches, staring out of the painting. It had long whiskers, dark green eyes, and a good long tail curled around in front of its paws. Sister Agatha lowered her fork to her plate; the *hmmmm* stopped before it could achieve its natural fade. The others looked over at the painting. Rachel was the last to put down her fork and raise her head.

"Look," Sister Martha said, "a cat has come for supper."

They all stared at the painting, at the cat, just as the cat stared at them. "She's looking right at us," Sister Felicity said.

Rachel said nothing. She went back to her pancakes.

"What made you think to put her in? The cat?" Sister Felicity asked.

Rachel finished the mouthful she was eating, then said, "To distract us from our own unbearable love."

No more questions were asked. One by one, each of them went back to eating her breakfast. Gradually the conversation resumed, but less animated than before.

When Sister Agatha drove the station wagon up to the walkway that led to the mansion door, each of the Sisters—who had already gathered in the great hall (empty now and vast)—picked up her suitcase and, inevitably, an auxiliary shopping bag (except for Sister Cathrael, who had a backpack which she slung onto one shoulder). They had bundled up warmly, with Sister Martha pulling Sister Felicity's scarf up over her mouth and nose because Felicity was the youngest and the smallest.

Stamping their booted feet against the cold floor even before they went out the door, the sisters seemed like a herd of eager ponies, impatient for release. When Sister Agatha opened the outside door, Sister Martha and Sister Cathrael laughed at the absurdity of the frost that slapped against their faces, leaving almost no sting at all, it was that cold. Giggling, testing to see how much steam they could force from their mouths, they tiptoed, pranced, and waddled down the shoveled walk to the waiting station wagon. The smoking exhaust seemed to promise warmth, and they hurried toward it.

Sister Felicity was the first to stop on the walkway and turn around. In comic succession, each bumped against the one in front of her until they had all come to a—literally—squealing halt. Sister Cathrael pretended to have been hurt by Sister Angela's suitcase when it knocked against her leg, and Sister Martha hauled her shopping bag onto her shoulder to keep it from getting crushed. One by one, each became silent.

Sister Agatha was still at the front door, bent forward, struggling with the key. The cold had frozen the lock, and it was refusing to work. Sister Agatha kept wiggling the key back and forth as if trying to bore her way in. Sister Martha lowered her bag. A few feet were stomped, then that too stopped. Unmoving, they watched as Sister Agatha, her ungloved hand struggling with the key, kept trying to complete the last act required of them by the house they had called "Mother." No one paid the least attention to the snow heavily falling, filling the folds of their scarves, cresting the shoulders of their coats, melting against whatever lay across the tops of their shopping bags. The great house, it seemed, refused to yield them up. Still, they would wait without impatience, without sound, for the click to come, announcing that they had finally left the house to itself, already consigned to the crowbar, the sledgehammer, and the wrecking ball.

Finally the key clicked in the lock, and a cheer went up, followed by another chorus of giggles to ridicule their worry over the lock. Sister Agatha came toward them, holding up the key like a found coin. Then, with a wide fling of her arm, she threw it up over the snowbank that lined the walkway.so it might fall on untouched snow.

After a few shouts of congratulation and approval, the Sisters continued toward the station wagon, knocking against each other, shortening their steps, huddling their way, their baggage catching onto handles not their own. So thick, so fast was the snow that the exhaust from the station wagon's tailpipe was no longer distinguishable among the falling flakes. Down the path the Sisters bustled.

Lining themselves along the side of the wagon, stamping their feet as if to hold down the snow, they waited for Sister Agatha to unlock the back of the wagon so they could stow their baggage. Rachel, standing at the passenger side, watched the steam rise up from among them, losing its way in through the relentless snow. She saw the sorry luggage they clutched, the stuffed belongings they were taking with them into exile. She saw a mist forming on Sister Angela's glasses, the swatch of white hair escaping from Sister Cathrael's head scarf, the mend on the thumb of Sister Felicity's glove, brown thread instead of navy blue. She stepped back, away from the huddle. She could see the tape on the handle of Sister Martha's suitcase and the familiar green woolen skirt covering the top of Sister Angela's shopping bag, soaking up the snow.

"My dear Sisters," Sister Felicity said. "My dear, dear Sisters, we are dispersed now, and never again will we meet as the community we have been. Our beloved Order is dissolved and is no more. We are going forth, which it has always been our calling to do. Let us, before we are gone from each other forever, let us say one more time the prayer that is our own."

There was only a slight silence, then the words began, low, except for Sister Martha who always had a high-pitched voice. "My soul gives glory to the Lord and my spirit rejoices in God my Savior..." The murmuring, the mumbling continued, the voices soft. "For he has regarded the humility of his handmaid, for behold, from henceforth, all generations shall call me blessed...."

Rachel tried to speak the words. Except for the Sisters near to her, she could see nothing. Even the Sisters themselves seemed a gathering of ghosts. Rachel could make out neither the great stone house nor the trees on the slope to the river. She could not see where the elms had stood, the place where she had said goodbye to her grandmother and her grandfather, to her brother George and her brother Phillip, and had kissed them. She could not see the rising chimneys and the high stone towers and the great window whose blades of light had transfigured Mother in her arms. She could not see the fountain where the summer birds had come.

Still the murmuring continued. "And His mercy is from generation to generation...." Rachel looked upward, into the snow. The snow was no longer falling. It was rising. The flakes were streaming upward, from earth to sky.

She had rescued no one. No one had she saved, no one had she ransomed with her love. Yet she had been given the gift of grief and never could it be taken from her. She had been allowed to mourn without ceasing, the weight heavy in her belly and on the lids of her eyes, her sorrow firm along the line of her jaw. And, for no moment that she could remember had she lived with a heart that was less than full. Upward the flakes were drawn, upward the words. For Rachel, standing there, everything was praise, was praise, was praise.

"... For He that is mighty hath done great things for me and holy is His name...."

She whispered the words so as not to disturb the rising snow.

ACKNOWLEDGMENTS

The author wishes to thank Yaddo and the members of its incomparable staff who, during the time this novel was written, provided him with more—much more—than bread.

He is also grateful to those friends who contributed their criticisms, their encouragement, and their counsel, including Don Ettlinger, Daniel D'Arezzo, Henri Cole, Eileen Simpson, Rebecca Stowe, Jay Rogoff, and David Barbour. To his nephew Jim he offers a special thanks for his gifted help in transferring the edited manuscript from typeface to computer. And an equally heartfelt thanks to his brother-in-law Tom Smith, who brought an editor's eye to a reading of the transferred copy.

And, of course, for his tenacious and persevering agent, Wendy Weil, and her equally steadfast assistant, Emily Forland, a gratitude beyond measure.

THE AUTHOR

Playwright and novelist, **Joseph Caldwell** was born and raised in Milwaukee, Wisconsin, but has lived the greater part of his life in New York City. He is the author of four previous novels: *The Uncle from Rome, Under the Dog Star, The Deer at the River,* and *In Such Dark Places.* He twice held the John Golden Fellowship in Playwriting at Yale University's School of Drama, and was awarded The Rome Prize in Literature by the American Academy of Arts and Letters.

Jonathan Santlofer